Chapter 1

"Jack?"

"Yes, my sweet?"

"Don't give me *'my sweet'*. Where's the bread?"

"Isn't it in the bread bin?"

"It's empty."

"Oh yeah. I remember now. I had a sandwich last night, before I turned in."

"And used the last two slices? The two I'd earmarked for my toast this morning?"

"I didn't notice a 'reserved' sign on them."

"What am I supposed to do now?"

"Cornflakes?"

"I had my heart set on toast."

"Sorry." He gave me a quick peck on the lips. "Got to rush. I have an early meeting."

"What about my toast?" I called after him, but he was already through the door.

"What's wrong, Jill?" Barry said.

"I'm sharing my life with a selfish man."

"Shell fish? What kind of shell fish?"

"No, not—never mind. Oh, well, if I want toast, I suppose I'll have to—"

I caught myself just in time. If I'd mentioned going out, Barry would have been at me to take him for a walk. I didn't have time for that, and besides, Jac y taken him out that morning. I threw a cou ,, Barry's favourite treats, into the kitchen, and 1 my coat and hurried outside.

"Morning, Jill!" Mrs Rollo was in her front

"Morning."

"Off to work?"

"Not just yet. I have to nip down to the shop. You're out and about early, today."

"I'm so excited I just can't settle. I barely slept a wink last night."

"Why's that?"

"My brother is coming over for a visit. He arrives later today."

"That's nice. Does he live far from here?"

"In Australia."

"Gosh. How long is it since you last saw him?"

"Almost eight years. He'll be staying with me for a few days, and then travelling around the country."

"That's great. I look forward to meeting him. Sorry, but I have to dash."

***

There was no sign of Toby Jugg or his wife, Judy, behind the counter of The Corner Shop.

"Good morning, young lady!" the middle-aged man with a ruddy complexion greeted me.

"Morning. Are Toby and Judy on holiday?"

"Didn't you know? They sold up and left."

"Really? I had no idea."

"From what I heard, Judy wasn't very happy with the life of a shopkeeper."

"I assume you'll be changing the shop's name? It's not exactly very imaginative."

"No, I'm definitely keeping the name. In fact, that's what attracted me to the shop in the first place. I knew as soon as I saw it that it was meant to be." He offered his hand. "I should introduce myself. My name is Jack. Jack Corner."

"Corner? Oh? I see what you mean about the shop name."

"Destiny, eh?"

Suddenly, he shrank in height by at least a foot. It was only then that I realised he must have been standing on a box. I guessed that made him *Little* Jack Corner.

I laughed at the thought.

"Sorry?" He came around the counter and stood beside me.

"Nothing. I was just thinking about something my dog said."

"Your dog?"

Whoops!

"Did I say dog? I meant neighbour."

Jack Corner looked confused. I seemed to have that effect on people.

"I'm Jill Gooder. I live just up the road."

"Pleased to meet you, Jill. What can I get for you, today?"

"Let me think. I'm okay for pudding, and for pie. Just a loaf of bread, please. Oh, and perhaps a packet of custard creams. Make that two packets."

"I adore custard creams."

I was warming to the little man—nursery rhyme name or not.

He took my money, and I was just on my way out when he called me back.

"I always like to share a thought for the day with my customers."

"Oh? Go on then."

"A bird in the hand is a silver lining."

Huh? "Okay, thanks for that. Bye, then."

On my way back home, I was conflicted. Should I go ahead with my original plan of toast for breakfast, or should I have a custard cream boost to set me up for the day?

"Mrs Mopp?"

She was waiting for me at the house when I got back.

"I didn't realise it was your day to clean."

"It isn't." She followed me inside. "I want a word."

"Would you like a drink?"

"No. This won't take long. I just wanted to let you know that I won't be cleaning for you anymore."

"Why not?"

At that moment, Barry came charging downstairs, and almost flattened me.

"Because of *that thing*!" She gestured to the dog.

"He didn't bite you, did he?"

"I'd never bite anyone." Barry turned to me. "I don't bite."

"Sorry, I know you don't."

"I don't what?" Mrs Mopp looked confused. "No, he didn't bite me, but I didn't sign up to clean a house with a dog. Dog hairs get everywhere."

"I suppose we could always pay a little more."

"No. My mind is made up. I'm sorry, but you'll have to make alternative arrangements."

And with that, she left.

"I don't think she likes me," Barry said.

"She doesn't like anyone. She's a funny woman."

"I don't like it here, Jill. I like the other place better."

"You have to give it a chance. I'm sure you'll grow to love it."

"I miss the park. And Babs. I miss Lucy and Hamlet too. I'm all by myself here."

"You've got me and Jack."

"You're out most of the time, and I don't think Jack likes me. "

"Of course he does."

"He never talks to me."

"I've told you. That's because he's a human."

"What's a human?"

Oh boy!

"Please, Jill. I want to go back to the other house. Can I? Can I, please?"

"I — err — I have to go to work now. We'll talk about this tonight."

"Promise?"

"I promise. But not while Jack is around."

Why did my life have to be so complicated?

In the end, I tossed a coin, and custard creams won. Tea and a custard cream for brekkie? Did it get any better than that? Actually, yes it did. How about tea and four custard creams?

Who are you calling greedy?

While I was munching on number three, the newspaper headline caught my eye. Despite my protests, Jack insisted on buying The Bugle once every week, for the bowling scores. Sad, I know.

'Dead Fall!'

The story related to a skydiver who had plunged to his death when his parachute had failed to open. A cold shiver ran down my spine as I recalled how close Peter had come to a similar fate. On that occasion, I'd been able to come to his rescue with a combination of magic and a haystack. Dale Thomas hadn't been so lucky. Apparently, he and his wife, who were both experienced skydivers, jumped together that day. What an awful experience for her.

***

It was Jules' day in the office. She appeared to be away with the fairies.

"Morning, Jules."

"Sorry, Jill. I was miles away."

"Is everything okay?"

"I'm worried about Gilbert."

"What's happened?"

"Nothing, really. It's like you said the other day — he's been acting rather strangely."

"Strange how?"

"He's usually quite chatty, but these last few days, he — err —" She hesitated. "Maybe it's just my imagination."

"Go on. What were you going to say?"

"He barely speaks, and when he does, it's like talking to a robot. I think he may have lost interest in me. He's probably got other women chasing after him now."

"Now he's not spotty you mean?"

"I suppose so."

"I don't think it's that. He seemed really sweet on you."

"So why has he changed?"

"Maybe it has something to do with his new job? When I saw him at the mall, he didn't look very happy at all."

"Perhaps you're right. Do you think I should say

something to him?"

"Why don't you leave it for a while, and see if he snaps out of it?"

"Yeah, that might be best. Thanks, Jill."

I didn't want to say any more to Jules, but my suspicionometer had been in the red zone ever since I'd first heard about Magical Skincare.

What? Never mind what the dictionary says. Of course suspicionometer is a real word.

It was time I took a closer look at the miracle acne treatment. I was pretty sure that magic was involved, and I was almost certain it was somehow responsible for Gilbert's sudden personality change.

"Good morning, Jill." Winky greeted me with a huge smile.

That was very disconcerting because normally, when I walked into the office in the morning, he was either fast asleep or demanding food.

"Morning?" I glanced around. He was obviously up to something.

"How was your weekend?"

"Err—fine. Just the usual." He never asked about my weekends. Something was definitely amiss.

"And Jack? How is he?"

"Enough! What are you up to?"

"Whatever do you mean?"

"You're up to something. What have you done, this time?"

"Nothing." His smile evaporated. "And frankly, I'm disappointed that you'd doubt my sincerity. We have to share this office, so it's only right that we should take an interest in one another."

"If it looks like a duck, and it sounds like a duck, then it's almost always a duck."

"Now you've lost me. What do ducks have to do with anything?"

"I know you, Winky. You're up to something, and when I find out what it is, there'll be trouble."

He sighed, and turned away. "I'm hurt. Truly hurt."

What do you mean, I'm cruel? You didn't fall for that old flannel, did you? Sheesh, I thought you would have known him better by now.

My phone rang. It was Kathy.

"Jill, I've been thinking."

Never a good sign. "Oh?"

"You and I don't spend nearly enough time together."

That was a matter of opinion. "Oh?"

"We used to chat for hours on end before I had the kids. These days, it seems like we only get the chance to grab a few words here and there."

"Oh?"

"*Oh?* Is that all you can say?"

"I'm just wondering where this is leading? What do you want?"

"Well, that's charming. Your problem, Jill, is you assume everyone has an agenda."

I glanced at Winky who was still sulking. Maybe Kathy was right. Perhaps, I was too quick to judge.

"Sorry. I've just had a bad start to the day."

"Why? What's happened?"

"Jack ate the last two slices of bread, which I'd planned to use for my toast this morning."

"That's it?"

"Of course not. Our cleaner has quit."

"Why?"

"She doesn't like the dog."

"Barry? What's not to like about him? He's a big, soft darling."

"Mrs Mopp doesn't share your views. And *he's* not happy here either."

"The dog? How do you know?"

"Just intuition, I guess."

"Okay. I'll forgive you this time, Miss Grumpy. Anyway, as I was saying, we should spend more time together. I was thinking that we could have a sisters' night. Pete's got a night out arranged with an old school friend. I could ask his mother to take the kids, and we could have a night in."

"Wouldn't you rather go out somewhere?"

"I was originally going to suggest that, but we wouldn't get a chance to talk properly because everywhere is so noisy these days. I thought we could stay in with a bottle of wine and lots of chocolates, and talk about old times."

I quite liked the sound of the wine and chocolates. The talk about old times, not so much.

"What do you say?" She pressed.

"Sure. Why not?"

I had a horrible feeling that I'd live to regret those words.

"Winky!"

He was on the sofa with his back to me.

"What?" he said, without looking around.

"I'm sorry."

"Sorry? I didn't quite hear that."
"I said I'm sorry."
"I almost heard you that time."
"Don't push your luck, buddy."

Chapter 2

Jules came through to my office.

"Jill, there's a Mr Carver here. He doesn't have an appointment, but he said he was given your name by a Mr Bob Dale."

I'd worked on a case when Bob Dale's stepdaughter had been kidnapped.

"Did he say what it was about?"

"Something about skydiving."

"Okay, Jules, show him in, would you?"

"Thank you for seeing me without an appointment." Mr Carver was tall, dark, but not particularly handsome.

"You know Bob Dale?"

"We've been friends for more years than I care to remember." He glanced across at Winky who was on the sofa, washing himself. "I had a cat just like that."

I seriously doubted it. "Really?"

"Yeah. Same colouring and only one eye. I used to call him Winky."

Was this some kind of windup?

"That's his name, too."

"No way. That's unbelievable." He walked over to Winky and began to stroke him.

Winky lapped up the attention. He jumped off the sofa, and began to rub against Carver's legs.

"My Winky went out one day, and never came back." Carver sighed. "I still miss that little rascal. The resemblance is remarkable. Where did you get him?"

"I've had him since he was a kitten," I lied.

"I can't get over the likeness."

"My receptionist said you wanted to talk to me about something to do with skydiving?"

"Yes." He gave Winky a final tickle under the chin, and then took a seat opposite me at the desk.

Winky still had his purring set to max volume, so I could barely hear myself think.

"Is it connected to the story I saw in The Bugle?" I asked.

"Yes, it is. Dale, the deceased, is—err—was a friend of mine. My best friend, actually. We'd known one another since we were kids."

"The Bugle's story said it was a tragic accident."

"I don't buy that. That's why I came to see you."

"But didn't it only happen a few days ago? The police can't have concluded their enquiries yet."

"Officially, they haven't, but it's obvious they've already made up their minds that it was an accident. Either that or suicide."

"There was no mention of suicide in the newspaper."

"There will be soon enough. The parachute didn't open, but the tests show it wasn't faulty. According to them, Dale hadn't pulled the cord, which means either he blacked out, or chose not to pull it."

"Aren't they the most likely explanations?"

"I suppose it's possible he blacked out. But, suicide? Never. No way."

"Do you think there might have been foul play?"

"I don't know. That's what I'd like you to find out, but you'll need to do it now, before the trail goes cold. Can you get straight onto it?"

I was working on precisely zero cases at that moment, but I didn't want to sound too eager. "I might be able to squeeze it in."

"I'd be so grateful. Bob told me what a wonderful job you did when Amanda was kidnapped. When could you start?"

"Wouldn't you like to know my fees first?"

"Money is no object."

Sweet music to my ears.

"Okay, then. Maybe I should start by asking you a few questions. Before we begin, can I get you a drink?"

"A coffee would be nice. Black, no sugar. Is there a toilet I can use?"

"Out through the main office, and along the corridor. It's the second on your left."

While Carver was paying a visit, I organised the drinks with Jules. Thankfully, her balancing skills had improved dramatically over recent months. Spillages were at an all-time low.

"Why did you lie to him?" Winky said.

"About what?"

"You said I'd been with you since I was a kitten."

"Oh, that? That was nothing."

"He looks familiar."

"Who does?"

"Your new client. I feel like I know him from somewhere."

"I imagine all humans look the same to a cat."

"Of course they don't. No, there's something decidedly familiar about him."

Fortunately, Carver came back just at that moment.

"Thanks for the coffee." He took a sip. "Where would you like to start?"

"You said that you and Dale were best friends? Do you skydive too?"

"Me?" He smiled. "I hate flying. It's all I can do to get onto a plane. I'm certainly never going to jump out of one. Dale was always the daredevil—even as a kid."

"Had he been skydiving long?"

"For at least fifteen years. He had hundreds of jumps under his belt."

"Could he have become complacent?"

"Never. He was a stickler for detail, and never cut corners when it came to safety. And besides, like I said, the parachute was found to be in perfect working order, but the cord hadn't been pulled."

"The article said he'd jumped with his wife?"

"That's right. Lesley is almost as experienced as Dale. They often jumped together."

"Was their marriage solid?"

"I'm not sure. I got the feeling that they might have been having a few problems."

"He told you that?"

"Not in so many words. I just got that vibe. Lesley is his second wife. His first, Patricia, died about fourteen years ago—cancer—quite tragic."

"Had he been acting differently recently?"

"Not really—same old Dale."

"I'll need to speak to his wife, and to whoever was piloting the aircraft that day. Is there anyone else you think I should talk to?"

"Dale had a difficult relationship with his son, Shane. From what I hear, he never really accepted his stepmother. And I believe that Dale and his brother, Philip, had had some kind of falling out."

"Okay. What about his business? Was it doing okay?"

"He never really discussed it, but yeah, as far as I know, everything was alright. You should speak to Robert Lane. He's Dale's partner. He's a skydiver too. In fact, I have a photograph of the three of them." Carver took out his phone. "There, that's Dale on the left with Lesley and Robert, on one of their skydiving jaunts."

"That's probably enough to be going on with. If you leave your contact details with my receptionist on the way out, I'll be in touch as soon as I have anything to report."

***

By the time my new client had left, Winky was fast asleep on the sofa. Was it possible that my one-eyed, darling cat had once belonged to Carver? And if he had, what should I do about it? As much as he drove me crazy, I'd hate to give Winky up. Maybe it was just a coincidence?

"This came while you were with that client." Jules passed me a flyer.

Coffee Triangle's 'Big' Day!

I gave it a quick glance. "It doesn't give much detail."

The flyer said little more than that they would be holding their 'Big' day in three days' time.

"Maybe it means you can 'go large' for free on that day," Jules suggested.

Go large? I hated that stupid phrase. Why can't people just say: *would you like a large cup?* No one ever says: *do you want to go small?* Do they?

"How exciting. Not!" I screwed up the flyer, and threw it into the bin.

"Shall I take away these cups, Jill?"

"Yes, please. And well done on the coffee. Not a single spillage."

"Thanks."

My phone rang.

"I'd better take this."

Jules grabbed the cups, and went back to the outer office.

"Aunt Lucy?"

"Jill, can you get over here straight away? There's something I think you need to see."

"What?"

"No time to explain. Come now or you'll miss it."

I magicked myself over to Aunt Lucy's house. She was in the lounge, staring at the TV. That in itself was unusual. I couldn't remember ever seeing her watch TV before. In fact, it seemed that very few people in the sup world bothered with it.

"Look!" Aunt Lucy pointed.

On screen, a young witch with red hair was about to interview a man whose face had been deliberately obscured so he couldn't be recognised.

"Welcome to Candle Investigates. My name is Eileen Clare."

E. Clare? Seriously?

"Today we will be discussing unusual goings-on at the sup world's most prestigious school: Candlefield Academy of Supernatural Studies or CASS, as it's more commonly known. In the studio with me is a man who I will refer to as Mr X. Mr X has requested that we do not divulge his identity." She turned to face the mystery man.

"Mr X, would you tell the viewers, in your own words, exactly what happened at CASS?"

"Certainly, Eileen." The man's voice had been distorted so he sounded like a robot. "The school is protected by a high wall, and a number of other anti-dragon defences. However, on this particular day, the wall was breached by a pouchfeeder."

For the benefit of the viewers, a photo of a pouchfeeder was displayed momentarily on-screen. The sight of the beast sent a shiver down my spine, as I remembered how close Tommy Bestwick had come to meeting a grisly end.

Mr X continued. "The pouchfeeder had grabbed one of the pupils—a young boy. It had the boy in its pouch, and was headed back to the breached section of wall. If it had got out, it would have been curtains for the boy."

"But that didn't happen?" Eclair prompted.

"No, thank goodness. He was saved by Jill Gooder."

"For the benefit of any viewers who may not already know, Jill Gooder turned down the opportunity to become the first ever level seven witch. Sorry to interrupt you, Mr X. Now, tell me, wasn't there something unusual in the manner in which Jill Gooder rescued the boy?"

"There was. At first it seemed to be a lost cause because there was no way to get to the breached section of wall in time to intercept the creature, but then Jill took a shortcut through a passageway which led straight to that section of the building."

"Surely, that was a sensible thing to do?"

"Of course, but the thing is that no one at CASS knew the secret passageway existed."

"Are you sure? No one?"

"I'm positive. And yet, Jill went straight to it."

By now, I'd worked out that the man in the studio must be one of the two wizards who had helped Tommy out of the pouchfeeder's pouch.

"How do you explain that?" Eclair asked.

"I can't. Everyone at the school was talking about it for days afterwards; no one understands what happened."

"Thank you, Mr X." Eclair turned to face the camera. "So, viewers, what are we to make of that? How could Jill Gooder, who supposedly had never visited CASS before, have known about the secret passageway? But, perhaps the more important question is: who is Jill Gooder? The story goes that she was raised in the human world—totally oblivious to the fact that she was a witch. In less than two short years, since discovering the truth, she has gone from zero to level seven. Remarkable. Or is it? Is there more to this story than Jill Gooder would have us know? We at Candle Investigates believe that the people of Candlefield deserve answers, and we intend to get them."

With that piece of theatre, the closing credits rolled.

"What was that all about?" I stared at the screen in disbelief.

"It was first broadcast last night," Aunt Lucy said. "The reruns are being shown every few hours."

"I don't understand what she was trying to insinuate. It's as though she thinks I have something to hide."

"I've never liked that woman." Aunt Lucy turned off the TV. "It seems to me she just likes to cause trouble."

"What do you think I should do?"

"What can you do? Ignore it—I would. It'll all be forgotten inside a week."

"You're probably right. While I'm here, there's

something I want to ask you. It's about Barry."

Chapter 3

When I arrived home, my neighbour, Megan Lovemore, had just pulled onto her drive. Megan was still juggling her twin roles as a model and gardener.

"Hi, Jill. You're home early."

"Yeah. I figured I deserved an early finish. How's the gardening business coming along?"

"Absolutely great. I've been asked to tender for providing regular maintenance to Washbridge House."

"Really?" Washbridge House was the nearest thing that Washbridge had to a stately home. I'd visited there a few times—the gardens were huge. "Are you equipped to handle a contract like that?"

"I know what you're thinking. It's too big a job for me to take on. I thought the same thing. I would never have dreamed of submitting a tender, but then Quentin called me, and suggested I do it."

"Quentin?"

"Quentin Rathbone. He's the owner's eldest son, and heir to the estate."

"I see. How do you know him?"

"We used to date. It was a couple of years ago, but we still keep in touch. He said I'd be in with a good chance. If I do land the contract, I'll have to recruit a lot of staff."

"Well, good luck with it."

"Thanks, Jill."

All through dinner, I could sense that Jack had something on his mind. I figured it must be to do with work, so didn't press him. Besides, I needed to talk to him about Barry, and to be perfectly honest, I wasn't looking forward to it.

After dinner, we went through to the lounge.

"There's something we need to talk about," we both said in almost perfect unison.

"You go first," he said.

"No. You, please."

"Okay. Look, I realise it was my idea in the first place, but I think Barry was a mistake." Jack could barely make eye contact with me.

"You can't call Barry a mistake!"

"That's not what I meant. *He* isn't a mistake, but having him here was. He's just too much. Do you think we might be able to find him a more suitable home?"

"I suppose I could always check back with the people I got him from to see if they could rehome him."

"I'll do it if you like. After all, it's my fault."

"That's okay. They know me. I'll speak to them."

"You seem to be taking this awfully well, Jill. I thought you'd explode."

"Me? Why would I? Aren't I always the epitome of calm?"

It would be difficult to accurately describe the look on Jack's face.

"What was it *you* wanted to talk about?" he asked.

"Me—err—I forget. Oh, wait. Mrs Mopp handed her notice in this morning."

"Why?"

"Who knows why that woman does anything? I tried to get her to reconsider, but her mind was made up."

"To be honest, I won't be sorry to see the back of her. I don't think she's ever forgiven me for asking about the ironing. What are we going to do?"

"*We* aren't going to do anything. Seeing as I have to relocate the dog, you can take responsibility for finding a new cleaner. You could start by putting an ad in the window of the corner shop."

"I can do that. In fact, I'll do it now. Strike while the iron is hot."

"It's under new ownership by the way. A little man by the name of Jack Corner." I laughed. "Little Jack Corner."

"I don't get it."

Sheesh! "Never mind. I'll make a phone call about Barry while you're down there."

I waited until Jack had left the house, and then went to see Barry who was asleep on the landing—Mrs Rollo had worn him out with a walk around the village.

"Barry! Wake up!"

"I'm tired."

"Wake up!"

"I'm too tired to walk."

"I have news. You can go back to the other place."

"I can?" He leapt to his feet. "To the park, and Babs?"

"Yep."

"When?"

"In the morning."

"Thanks, Jill." He planted his paws on my chest, and gave me a sloppy lick. Yuk!

"Mr Corner really is tiny, isn't he?" Jack said when he got back from the shop.

"Did he have his thumb in a pie?"

"Sorry?"

"Never mind. I've made a call, and they're happy to

take Barry back. They said they have just the home for him."

"They do? That's great. I have to say, Jill, you've taken this remarkably well."

"I'm disappointed, obviously, but your happiness is the most important thing in my life."

What? Too much? I don't think so — you've got to milk it for all it's worth.

***

The next morning, Barry was on my case as soon as I got up.

"When are we going, Jill? I want to see Babs. I want to go to the park."

"He's even more excitable than usual," Jack commented, on his way to the kitchen. "It's as though he knows."

"Calm down," I said to Barry. "We'll go as soon as Jack's gone to work."

"Did you say something?" Jack called from the kitchen.

"No. Just talking to the dog."

As soon as Jack was out of the door, I magicked myself and Barry over to Aunt Lucy's house.

"I'm back!" He jumped onto the sofa, next to Aunt Lucy, and began to lick her face.

"It's good to have you back, boy. I've missed you."

"Can we go to the park? Can we? I love the park."

"Come on then." She took his lead. "Do you want to come with us, Jill?"

"No, thanks. I thought I'd drop in at Cuppy C."

"For a muffin?"

"Hmm? I hadn't thought about that, but now you come to mention it—"

"Barry!" Lester came into the room. "Good to have you back, boy!"

The big soft dog bounded over to him.

"Is the training still going okay?" I asked Lester.

"Apart from the body snatchers."

"They're still at it?"

"Oh, yes. It's getting ridiculous. There have been dozens of bodies snatched now. Monica says she's never known anything on this scale before."

After I'd said my goodbyes, I went in search of blueberry muffinness.

As soon as I walked into Cuppy C, I realised that several people were staring at me.

"Have I got something on my face?" I asked Pearl.

"No. Why?"

"They're all staring at me."

"It's because of that TV programme," Pearl said. "Haven't you seen it?"

"I saw it at Aunt Lucy's."

"Everyone's talking about it," Amber said.

"Great."

"Lots of people have asked us about you today."

"What did you tell them?"

"That there was nothing to tell. We said you were just a regular witch." Pearl hesitated. "Who just happened to go from zero to level seven in no time at all."

"And who can sniff out hidden passageways." Amber grinned.

"Thanks very much, you two. I should have known I could rely on you to be discreet. Can I get a coffee and a blueberry muffin?"

"Do you want to go large?"

"When did you start with the *going large* nonsense? Just give me a regular."

"Isn't that what they say in the human world?"

"It's not what *I* say."

"We're getting genned up for our weekend in London." Amber passed me the coffee.

"I'd forgotten about that. Have you booked it yet?"

"No," Pearl said. "We wanted to talk to you first."

"Me? Why?"

"We thought you might like to come with us?"

"Go with you?" I almost spat out the coffee. "Why would you want me to tag along?"

"It turns out there's a special offer on the accommodation and rail package."

"Won't you just magic yourselves there?"

"No. We want the full experience. We're going to get a train from Washbridge. And it turns out there's a special offer: Three for the price of two."

Three for two, eh? That meant I'd get to go for free. I hadn't been too keen on the idea of a weekend in London with the twins, but as it was free.

"Okay. I'll make up the numbers."

"Great. Sharing the cost three ways will make it much cheaper for us. Thanks, Jill."

"Sharing the cost?"

"Yeah."

"Three ways?"

"Yeah. It's going to be great, isn't it?"

"Great, yeah."

Just then, a man walked past us, and towards the stairs.
"Who was that?" I asked.
"That's Talbot. He's our lodger," Pearl said.
"I thought you weren't taking on any more tenants."
"This is different," Amber said. "It's just a short-term rental. A couple of weeks at the most. He came in for a coffee, and happened to mention that he was looking for somewhere to stay. It seemed silly to turn away the cash."
"What does he do?"
Amber shrugged.
"I don't know," Pearl said.
"Come on. You must know."
"He's some kind of salesman, I think." Amber picked at one of her nails.
Both of them were acting very shiftily.
"I'll go and ask him." I started towards the stairs.
"No, wait." Pearl grabbed my arm. "If you must know, he sells oils. Specialist oils."
"What kind of specialist oils?"
The twins exchanged a glance. "Animal oils."
"What kind of animal?"
"Alright!" Pearl said. "Snake oil. Satisfied?"
Priceless!

***

I was still chuckling to myself about the twins' snake oil salesman when I stepped out of Cuppy C.
My good humour didn't last long, though.
"Jill Gooder. Could we have a quick word?"

A TV camera was pointed at me, and a bright light was being shone in my eyes. I could barely see the woman who was holding a microphone under my nose. I recognised her voice though—it was Eclair.

"Get that camera away from me." I tried to push it away, but the cameraman took a step back so that he was beyond my reach.

"Jill, how did you know the location of the secret passageway at CASS?"

"I don't know. I just did."

"Do you really expect people to believe that?"

"I don't care what people believe. It happens to be the truth. Now, get that microphone and camera away from me."

"And do you still insist that you didn't even know you were a witch until you were in your twenties?"

"It's the truth."

"And yet, you managed to progress through the levels remarkably quickly."

"I've nothing else to say. Please move out of the way."

I might as well have been talking to a brick wall for all of the notice she took.

"Leave her alone!" Pearl was standing in the doorway.

"Yeah. Get away from here!" Amber shouted over her sister's shoulder.

"Are you two covering up for her?" The microphone and camera were turned onto the twins.

"Get back inside!" I shouted. "I can handle this."

The twins retreated back inside Cuppy C.

"Leave them alone," I barked at Eclair. "I'll answer your questions."

"Good, okay let's start—"

"But not here. If you want to interview me, it has to be in the studio, and I'll need to see a list of questions in advance."

"But what about—"

"That's it. Take it or leave it."

Eclair put the microphone down, and told the cameraman to stop filming.

"When can you come into the studio?" she asked.

"Let me have a list of questions, and I'll get back to you. Now, if you don't mind." I pushed past her.

***

For once, I was pleased to escape from Candlefield, and return to the human world. At least there, I was just regular 'Jill Gooder', and I didn't have to worry about someone pointing a TV camera at me.

The last thing I wanted to do was take part in some TV show, but it was the only way to get Eclair off my back. This whole affair had got me thinking about Imelda Barrowtop, and what she'd said to me on her deathbed. In her delusional state, she'd obviously mistaken me for Magna Mondale. But that wasn't what was playing on my mind. I kept thinking about the spell she'd asked me about. The 'double dark' spell. It must have been important for her to have used her last breath to ask about it. Had it been in the book? I didn't remember seeing it, but then I'd had only a limited amount of time to study the book before I'd been forced to cast it down the Dark Well.

For now, I had more pressing matters to attend to—like the skydiving case. I had arranged to visit the airfield later, to speak to the operator who had flown the plane from which Dale Thomas and his wife had jumped on that fateful day. But first, I was going to call in at the office to see if there was anything else which needed my attention.

Chapter 4

It was Mrs V's day in the office, and I could hear the sound of knitting needles clicking, even before I walked in.

"Morning, Mrs V."

Huh? The office was deserted. And yet, on her desk was a pair of needles which appeared to be knitting all by themselves. The scarf they were working on was already over two feet long.

"Mrs V? Are you there?" I said to the empty chair. Perhaps she had upset Grandma, who had retaliated by making her invisible. "Mrs V?" I applied maximum focus. If it was an invisibility spell, that should allow me to 'break through' it.

Nothing. Whatever this was, it wasn't the 'invisible' spell. Then, without warning, the needles stopped knitting. I picked them up and studied them carefully. As far as I could make out, they were just regular knitting needles. It made no sense whatsoever.

"Jill, sorry I'm late." A flustered Mrs V appeared in the doorway. "The bus was delayed."

"That's okay."

She walked over to her desk, and picked up the knitting. "It's coming along quite nicely, don't you think?" Mrs V held it up for my inspection.

"Very nice. Is the scarf longer than you'd expected?"

"What do you mean?"

"I—err—was just wondering. Does it seem longer than when you left it here, last night?"

"Of course it is. I've knitted another four inches this morning."

"This morning? Were you in earlier?"

"No. I just got here—you saw me." She gave me a puzzled look. "Are you okay, Jill?"

"I'm just a little confused. You said that you knitted four inches this morning, but you've only just arrived."

"I did it on the bus."

"Oh?" Now I was even more confused. "How did you do it on the bus when the scarf was on your desk?"

"It's your grandmother's latest invention."

I should have known. "I don't think I've heard about that."

"Your grandmother and I may have our differences, and I'm still not happy at the way she let me go, but there's no denying the woman is a genius when it comes to yarn innovation."

"What exactly is this new invention?"

"I'm trying to remember what it's called—White Tie Needles or something like that."

"And how does it work?"

"It's brilliant. You have two pairs of needles. You cast the wool onto one pair, and you use the other pair to knit with."

"I don't get it."

"It's really quite simple. This morning, I had the second pair of needles with me on the bus. I used them to go through the motions of knitting, and that caused the pair of needles on my desk to copy my actions."

"I don't see the point in that. Why don't you just knit in the conventional way on the bus?"

"Because then I'd have to carry the scarf back and forth between home and work. It can be difficult to manage large items of knitting in the confines of the bus. This way, all I need to carry is the needles, so there's no scarf for people to trip over. It's brilliant, don't you think?"

"I guess so, but how does it work?"

"I've just told you."

"I understand *what* it does. I just can't see *how* it does it."

"Don't ask me, dear." She laughed. "You know I'm not very technically minded. You should ask your grandmother."

"Oh, I intend to."

What on earth was wrong with Grandma? Not satisfied with flaunting magic with her Everlasting Wool and One-Size Needles, she had now introduced White Tie Needles. I needed to have a serious talk with that woman.

***

"What's that?" I pointed to the white box on my desk. Sitting next to it, and looking very pleased with himself, was Winky.

"It's for you. Take a look."

"Who brought it in?"

"It's from me. A present."

My suspicionometer was back in the red zone. "What is it?"

"Open it and find out."

I lifted the lid, gingerly. Inside, was a beautiful iced cake.

"What's this for?"

"Does there have to be a reason for me to bake you a cake?"

"What have you done?"

"Nothing."

"What are you planning to do, then?"

"Look, if you must know, I feel a little guilty about the misunderstanding over the nett and gross profit thing."

He'd tried to cheat me out of my share of the profits from his woolly jumper enterprise by manipulating the P&L report, but thanks to Luther, I'd sussed him out.

"Fair enough." I wasn't one to hold a grudge. "Where did you buy it?"

"I baked it myself."

I laughed. "No, seriously, where did you buy it?"

"I really did bake it. Do you want a slice now?"

"Okay, but only if you have some first."

"It's your cake. You should have the first piece."

"No. You first. I insist."

"Do you think I've poisoned it or something?"

"Of course not." I wouldn't have put anything past him.

After I'd seen Winky eat some and survive, I decided to give it a try. And, I have to admit, it was delicious. There was way too much of it for me to eat by myself, so I gave a slice to Mrs V.

"Mmmm, that's delicious." She wiped the crumbs from her lips. "Who made it?"

"I did." I could hardly tell her it was Winky, could I?

She laughed. "No, seriously, who made it? Was it that next-door neighbour of yours? Didn't you say she often gives you cakes?"

"You got me. Yes, it was Mrs Rollo."

It was coming to something when Mrs V was prepared to accept that Mrs Rollo, the world's worst baker, had made the cake, but couldn't believe that I might have made it.

***

I still had some time to kill before my appointment with the skydiving operator, so I took a walk down to Ever. On almost every lamp post between my office and the shop there were posters about Coffee Triangle's 'Big' Day. Once again, there was precious little detail about what exactly would be happening, but maybe that was all part of the plan. I was now sufficiently intrigued that I intended to pay them a visit on the day.

"Are we still on for tonight?" Kathy said. She was behind the counter at Ever.

"Yeah. Jack is going bowling with one of his sad friends."

"I hope you don't call them that in front of Jack."

"Of course not. You know me — diplomacy personified."

She rolled her eyes.

"What's with this White Tie Needles nonsense?" I asked.

"White tie?" Kathy shook her head.

"Mrs V was telling me about it. This new-fangled invention that Grandma has come up with that allows you to knit remotely."

"Oh, you mean Wi-Fi Needles."

"Do I?"

"It only launched a couple of days ago, but it's selling like hot cakes."

"How does it work?"

Kathy reached under the counter, and produced a pair of knitting needles. "Look over there." She pointed to another pair of needles at the far end of the counter.

"When I knit with these, those over there will mimic my movements."

To demonstrate, she began to go through the motions with the needles in her hands. As she did, the needles at the other end of the counter followed suit.

"Clever, isn't it?" she said.

"Very, but how does it work?"

"Wi-Fi."

"There's no internet connection in this shop." I took out my phone to double-check.

"There must be or it wouldn't work, would it?" Kathy shrugged.

"I suppose not. Is Grandma on the roof terrace?"

"No, she's in her office." Kathy leaned forward, and said in a hushed voice, "Last time I walked past the door, I could hear her snoring. She won't thank you for waking her up."

"I'll risk it."

Kathy was right. I could hear the snoring when I was still several feet from her office.

"Hi, Grandma!" I said, as I burst through the door.

She jumped so much that she almost fell out of her chair. "Do you have to come charging in here like that?"

"Sorry. If I'd realised you were asleep, I wouldn't have disturbed you." Snigger.

"I wasn't asleep. What did you want?"

"To talk to you about Wi-Fi Needles."

"My best invention to-date, wouldn't you say? Sales are through the roof."

"Why do you insist on calling it an invention? It's obviously magic."

"Says you, but then I wouldn't expect you to understand the complexities of digital networks."

"Do I look stupid? Don't answer that. You know as well as I do that this has nothing to do with Wi-Fi or digital networks. It's a blatant abuse of your magical powers."

"Even if that was true, and I'm not saying it is, why are you getting your knickers in such a twist?"

"Because you're going to get into trouble."

"Who with? Department V?" She cackled. "I don't think so."

"You think you're untouchable, don't you?"

"Pretty much. Now, was there something else? I have work to attend to."

"How did that go?" Kathy asked, on my way out.

"Don't ask. That woman is impossible."

Before she could say anything else, a customer approached the counter.

"Do you have those Wi-Fi Needles? My friend told me about them. They sound wonderful."

***

I was so busy grumbling to myself about Grandma and her stupid 'inventions' that I didn't spot Betty Longbottom until it was too late to avoid her.

"Hi, Jill. You look deep in thought. Is everything okay?"

"Yeah. It's just Grandma, driving me crazy as usual."

"She scares me."

"She scares most people. How's Norman?"

"Don't talk to me about that man. His bottle tops are taking over the shop. I've had to put half of my stock into storage."

"Are the bottle tops selling well, then?"

"Oh yes. The shop has turned into a magnet for every bottle top anorak in a fifty mile radius."

"That must be good for your profitability?"

"I guess so." She sighed. "I see that you're running a marketing campaign too. I can't say I get it though."

"What marketing campaign?"

"All those posters down the other end of the High Street." She pointed. "What's the significance of the witch's outfit?"

"The what? What do you mean?"

"I assumed you'd had the posters put up. They're pictures of you dressed in a witch's outfit."

"Sorry, Betty. I have to run."

I had to find those posters.

It wasn't difficult. They were pasted on every available surface. Each one had a cartoon image of a witch, with my face superimposed on it. The wording read: This Woman Is A Witch.

Who could have done this? My first thought was Ma Chivers. She had been responsible for messing with Grandma's advertising. But this was far worse. This threatened to blow my cover.

Don't panic, Jill. I tried to convince myself that there was nothing to worry about. No one would take the posters literally. Like Betty, they would just assume they were some kind of obscure marketing campaign. Even so, I wanted them gone, so I set about ripping them down one by one.

It had taken the best part of an hour, but I had finally reached what appeared to be the last one.

"Isn't that your face on the poster?" A man wearing a striped apron appeared out of the fishmonger's shop.

I tore it down. "It was someone's idea of a practical joke. Did you see who put them up?"

"Two young women."

"Are you sure it wasn't a woman and a man?" If it wasn't Ma Chivers, I would have expected it to be Alicia and Cyril.

"Of course I am. They were very pretty. I heard one of them call the other one Flora."

The Ice Maidens. What where they doing in Washbridge? And what was with the poster campaign? I suspected the answer to both of those questions was the same: Miles Best.

"Are you?" the fishmonger said.

"Am I what?"

"A witch?"

"Do I look like a witch?"

He studied me for a long moment. "You've got the nose for it."

"And you stink of fish, but that doesn't make you a mackerel, does it?"

That silenced him. He was obviously no match for my cutting wit.

Chapter 5

I was surprised to discover that there were two airfields in the Washbridge area: North and South. They were both small concerns, and used mainly by local skydiving clubs.

Gerry Southland was the owner of Skydiving Adventures. I found him tinkering with his plane, which was a horrible canary yellow colour.

"You must be Jill. Do come in." He showed me into a small office, which was adjacent to the only hangar on Washbridge South Airfield. "Sorry for the mess."

The office comprised of a desk, two chairs, and a sorry looking filing cabinet.

"Terrible business, this," he said, as he took a seat at the desk. "I've done this for almost seventeen years, and not so much as a broken leg until now."

"That's a pretty impressive record. I'd assumed you'd get a lot of injuries in this game."

"I don't take learners, and that's where most of the injuries occur. Everyone who jumps with me is an experienced skydiver. Much less hassle that way."

"Can you tell me what you remember about that day?"

"There was nothing out of the ordinary. The two customers knew what they were doing."

"They'd jumped with you before?"

"Actually, no. From what I understood, they had a friend with his own plane based at Washbridge North Airfield."

"Why did they come to you that day?"

"Apparently, their regular ride was in for repair."

"So, you'd never met Dale Thomas or his wife before then?"

"No, but they obviously knew what they were doing. When you've been in the game as long as I have, you can tell within five minutes of meeting someone."

"Do you have any theories about what might have gone wrong?"

"I understand the police think he may have blacked out?"

I nodded. "Or that it was suicide."

"I find that hard to believe."

"Why's that?"

"The man, Dale, was in a great mood—laughing and joking. He didn't strike me as a man who was about to commit suicide. A blackout seems the most likely explanation."

"Is there any possibility it could have been equipment failure?"

"Zero. I insist on double-checking the parachutes myself. Some of the old hands don't appreciate me doing it, but I tell 'em: *Either I check your parachute or you don't jump with me.* The guy's parachute was A-OK when he got on the plane. Isn't that what the police report said?"

"Yeah. They said the parachute was fine, but that the cord hadn't been pulled."

"He must have blacked out then. Poor guy. I feel for his missus too. It must have been horrible for her to see him plunge to his death."

"Did you see it?"

"No. I'm always long gone by the time they pull their cords. First I knew about it was when I heard the ambulance siren."

***

It was some time since I'd had the dubious pleasure of talking to Miles Best, and even longer since I'd been inside Best Cakes. The Ice Maidens were nowhere to be seen — neither were Miles or his girlfriend, Mindy.

"What can I get for you?" The young woman behind the counter was wearing an eye patch. Having seen Winky wear a wide variety of eye patches, I found this one to be quite plain by comparison. I considered telling her where she could find a better selection, but decided to mind my own business.

What do you mean, that must be a first?

"Are Flora and Laura in today?"

"No, sorry. It's their day off. I'm Nora. Can I help?"

Flora, Laura and now Nora? What was this? Rhyming dictionary corner?

"What about Miles or Mindy? Are they in?"

Before she could reply, Miles appeared from a door behind the counter. Mindy was by his side. "Hello, Jill. We don't see you in here very often. Are you after a better class of muffin? I believe you're partial to blueberry."

"I'm not here for a muffin."

"A cupcake, then?"

"I don't want anything to eat or drink. I came to see the Ice Maidens."

"Who?"

"Flora and Laura."

"You're out of luck, I'm afraid. It's their day off. Is there something I can help you with?"

"You can tell them that if they put up any more posters of me, they'll regret it."

"You seem rather upset. Are you sure you wouldn't like

a cup of tea? How about camomile? It might soothe your nerves."

"My nerves are perfectly fine, thank you. I just want to know what you think you're playing at with those posters? I know you're behind it."

"I have no idea what you're talking about. Look, I can see you're upset. Is all the TV exposure getting to you? I can see how it might."

"What's your game, Miles?"

"I don't know what you mean."

"Let me spell this out for you. If I find one more poster of me in Washbridge, I'll be back."

"What were you doing across the road, Jill?" Amber was behind the tea room counter in Cuppy C. Pearl was nowhere to be seen.

"Just having a quiet word with Miles."

"What's he done now?"

"Nothing worth worrying about. Where's Pearl?"

"Shopping for clothes for London. We tossed a coin, and she won. I get to go tomorrow. Have you bought yours yet?"

"Me? No. I hadn't planned on getting anything new."

"Your wardrobe could do with refreshing."

"Thanks."

"Sorry, but it's true. We don't want you to show us up."

"Could I get a top-up?" someone shouted from one of the window tables. It was the snake oil salesman.

"That's the seventh top-up he's had," Amber whispered.

"He's having a laugh. Why don't you tell him he has to pay?"

"I don't like to." Amber collected his cup, topped it up, and took it back to him.

"Young lady!" he called.

"He's talking to you." Amber nudged me.

"Would you care to join me?" He smiled a particularly untrustworthy smile.

"Sorry, but there's somewhere I have to be."

"It will only take a minute."

"Okay." If he tried to sell me his snake oil, he'd be sorry.

"I'm Talbot." He took my hand and planted a kiss on it. Yuk!

"Is that your first name or last name?"

"It's my only name. My mother insisted one name was enough for anyone. Can I get you a drink?"

"No, thanks. Like I said, I can't stay long."

"I believe your name is Jill?"

I nodded.

"I saw the Candle TV programme where they talked about you."

"You and everyone else, apparently."

"I may be able to help."

"Who says I need help?"

"Maybe you do. Maybe you don't. Tell me, what do you know about snake oil?"

Here we go. "That I'm not going to pay good money for it."

He laughed. "Your view is jaundiced by your experience in the human world. Snake oil has a bad rap over there. The oil from snakes here in the sup world is a completely different proposition."

"Of course it is."

"I can see you're sceptical."

"Like I said, I don't have much time."

"There are hundreds of different kinds of snakes in the sup world."

"I haven't seen any so far."

"You're unlikely to around here. They're found in the unpopulated regions — around CASS for example."

"You've been to CASS?"

"No, but I have my sources in that region. Anyway, as I was saying, there are numerous breeds of snake. The oil from each one has its own particular properties."

"That's really fascinating, but —"

"One in particular should be of interest to you."

"I seriously doubt that." I stood up. There was no way I was buying snake oil from this guy. Can you imagine how much grief I would have got from the twins if I had?

"The redsnap snake," he called after me. "It'll help with your memory."

Cheek of the man! There was nothing wrong with my memory.

***

That evening when I arrived at Kathy's, she came to the door barefoot, with her trousers rolled up to her knees.

"That's quite the look." I laughed. "Have you been for a paddle?"

"I'm glad you think it's funny. And yes, I have. The stupid washing machine decided to leak all over the kitchen floor. Of course, it waited until Pete had gone out, so muggins here had to sort it out by herself."

"What about the kids?"

"They were already at Pete's Mum's, thank goodness."

"I thought you'd only recently bought a new washing machine?"

"We have. It was only delivered four days ago. I shall be giving them a piece of my mind, in the morning. Why don't you get the wine out of the fridge while I go upstairs and get changed?"

"Isn't it still wet in the kitchen?"

"No. I've mopped it all up. I'll only be a minute."

Poor old Kathy.

The washing machine door was still wide open, and even I could see that the door seal looked as though it had perished. I made a mental note of the manufacturer's name: Elf Washing Machines. I'd be sure to avoid them the next time I needed a new one.

"What's Jack doing?" Kathy had changed, and joined me in the lounge.

"He's gone bowling with Trevor—one of his friends from work."

"I need this." She took a drink of wine. "I've had a lousy day."

"With the washing machine, you mean?"

"Not just that. Pete thought he'd landed a massive new contract, but then he got a call today to say they're going to look at another bid before deciding. It's for Washbridge House."

"Oh dear."

"What?"

"I think I might know who the other bidder is."

"Who?"

"Megan."

"How can she take on a contract of that size? It's big even for Pete, and he already has plenty of contacts who he can bring in."

"Apparently, she used to date the owner's son."

"Well that's just great! That woman will be the death of me."

It was just as well I'd travelled to Kathy's by taxi because two hours later, we were both well oiled.

"Do you remember when we used to collect Miss Makeup stickers?" Kathy laughed.

"I never collected Miss Makeup stickers."

"We both did."

"I don't think so."

"You had the one I needed to give me the complete set, but you wouldn't swap with me. Meanie!"

"That doesn't sound like me at all."

"You said you'd only let me have it if I gave you my beanies."

"If that is true, and I'm not saying it is, then I was only doing it to rescue those poor beanies from your clutches. You never did know how to look after them."

Kathy suddenly started to laugh uncontrollably.

"What's tickling you now?"

"I just remembered your penfriend. What was her name?"

"Rosy Glass."

"What a nutter."

"Rosy wasn't a nutter. She was nice."

"She used to collect ships in bottles."

"She sent me photos of them. They were nice." I laughed. "Stick insects too."

"What?"

"She used to keep stick insects."

"I don't remember that."

"I wonder what she's doing now."

"Wake up you two!"

I forced one eye open. Kathy was still asleep, with her head on my lap.

"Peter?" I managed through dry lips.

"Looks like you two have had a good time." He glanced at the empty bottle.

"Kathy!" I nudged her. "Wake up. Peter's home."

"Pete!" She sat up. "My handsome hunk. Give me a kiss."

"You're drunk, Kathy." He shook his head.

"No, I'm not." She hiccupped. "I know something you don't."

"What's that?"

"Little Miss Meggy Megs has bid for the Washbridge House job."

Peter turned to me. "Is that true?"

I nodded. "Seems she used to date the owner's son."

"And the washing machine's bust." Kathy stood up. "I'm going to bed."

"I'll call a taxi." I picked up my phone.

"It's okay, Jill," Peter said. "I'll give you a lift. *I* haven't had a drink."

Chapter 6

Never again! The next morning, my head felt like it was full of little men, all operating pneumatic drills.

"Full English?" Jack said when I eventually made it into the kitchen.

I was onto him; he never offered to make a fry-up during the week. He was only doing it because he knew I wouldn't be able to face it.

"No, thanks."

"How was Kathy?"

"Up to her ankles in water. Her new washing machine had sprung a leak."

"Oh dear. I don't imagine she was in a very good mood, then?"

"She wasn't best pleased. And you can just imagine how she reacted when I told her about Megan."

"I bet that went down well. What else did you two talk about all evening?"

"Oh, you know. This and that. Mainly ships in bottles and stick insects."

"Is that code for 'mind your own business'? "

"No. We got talking about a pen friend I had when I was a kid. She used to collect ships in bottles, and keep stick insects."

"She sounds even weirder than you, and I didn't think that was possible." He grinned.

"If I didn't have such a hangover, I'd thump you for that."

"By the way, I've found a new cleaner. Someone saw the ad that I'd posted in the corner shop, and phoned yesterday. She came around last night before I went bowling. She seems ideal, and has a much pleasanter disposition than Mrs Mopp."

"That wouldn't be difficult. What's her name?"

"Agatha."

"Agatha what?"

"Just Agatha."

"She must have another name."

"You'll make fun of it."

"When did I ever make fun of someone's name?"

"Her other name is Crustie."

"Agatha Crustie?" I dissolved into laughter.

"See! That's why I didn't want to tell you."

"Sorry." I could barely breathe; I was laughing so much.

"Don't you dare take the mickey out of her name when she's here. We don't want to lose another cleaner."

"But, it's Agatha Crustie!" My sides were hurting from laughing.

"Jill! You have to promise me."

"Okay, I promise." I wiped the tears from my eyes. "Agatha Crustie."

"The house seems empty without Barry." Jack sighed.

"It's no good feeling guilty now. You were the one who wanted to throw him out onto the streets."

"Thanks for not making me feel bad about it."

"I'm only joking. Barry will be much happier where he is. There's a park close by, and he'll have someone with him all day."

"You never actually said where you were taking him."

Whoops!

"It's just the other side of thingamabob. You know, near to whatdoyoucallit." I glanced at my watch. "Is that the time? I have to rush. I've got a meeting with whatshisname. See you, tonight."

That was another close call. It was getting more and more difficult to remember what I could and couldn't tell Jack. I could hardly have said: *Barry? Oh, I magicked him back to the sup world.*

If nothing else, all that laughing at our new cleaner's name had got rid of my headache. Who knew that laughter was a cure for a hangover?

"Jill!" Mrs Rollo shouted. She was standing next to a thickset man who had grey hair and a black beard.

"Morning, Mrs Rollo."

"Jill, this is my brother, Marco."

Do not laugh at his name, Jill. You mustn't laugh.

I laughed.

Both Mrs Rollo and her brother gave me a puzzled look.

"Sorry, I was just thinking about something Jack said."

"Hi." The man offered his hand. "Marco Rollo. Pleased to meet you."

I laughed again. "Sorry. Jack can be such a comedian. Nice to meet you — err — Marco."

"You too, Jill. Rita has told me a lot about you. She's lucky to have such a considerate neighbour. But then, I guess you must feel blessed to live next door to such a talented baker. I bet she keeps you stocked up with cakes, doesn't she?"

"She certainly does." Our bin is always full of them. "Mrs Rollo said you lived in Australia?"

"That's right. One heck of a journey it is too. Still, it's worth it to see Rita." He put his arm around his sister.

"That's not the only reason he came over, though," Mrs Rollo said. "Is it Marco? Tell Jill why you're here."

"Without wishing to blow my own trumpet, I'm

something of a leading light in the paranormal activity scene in Australia."

"Ghosts and stuff?"

"Among other things. Anyway, I've been invited to give a number of presentations around the UK. One of them is right here in Washbridge at PAW—you may have heard of it."

"I don't think so."

"It stands for Paranormal Activity Watch."

"I had no idea there was such a thing hereabouts."

"You might be surprised to hear that there are more reports of paranormal activity here in Washbridge than in any other town or city in the UK."

Not as surprised as you might think. "Really? That's unbelievable."

"I know," Mrs Rollo said. "Marco reckons we might even have witches and wizards living among us here in Smallwash. It's a bit spooky, isn't it?"

"Okay, you got me." I held up my hands. "I'm really a witch."

They both laughed.

Snigger.

* * *

I'd arranged to meet with Lesley Thomas, the widow of the dead skydiver, but I had a little time to kill before then, so thought I'd take a quick look at Magical Skincare who had one of the smaller units on the Speedlink Industrial Estate. I wanted to try to find out what had caused Gilbert's recent personality change, and this seemed as good a place as any to start.

I stood behind a low wall, across the road from the unit, from where I had a good view of all the comings and goings. Ten minutes after I arrived, a young woman appeared. To gain entry to the building, she had to enter a PIN into the number pad next to the door. At first, I thought it was one of the promotional staff I'd seen working alongside Gilbert at Central Mall, but then I realised it couldn't be. This poor young woman had terrible acne. There was no way she would have been put forward as one of the faces of Magical Skincare. A few minutes later, a young man arrived—he too had a severe case of acne. Next to arrive was Gilbert. He had the same 'out-to-lunch' expression as he'd had at the mall. But that wasn't what caught my eye. Gilbert's acne was back with a vengeance. It was every bit as bad as when Jules had first dated him. How could that be? Only a few days earlier, his complexion had been flawless.

There was no more activity for the next ten minutes. I'd have to be on my way soon or I'd be late for my appointment with Lesley Thomas. Just then, the door to Magical Skincare opened, and out came Gilbert, and the young man and woman who I'd seen go in just a few minutes before.

All three of them now had flawless skin.

Something very strange was going on inside that building, and I intended to return, to find out what.

***

Lesley Thomas looked more like a ghost than most of the 'real' ghosts I knew. She was pale and drawn, and her hair was dishevelled.

"Thank you for seeing me," I said.

"Come in. I apologise for my appearance. I haven't really been myself these last few days."

"That's understandable."

She led the way into the living room, and gestured for me to take the seat next to the patio doors.

"I know you probably told me on the phone, but I'm not sure what you need from me." Lesley sat in the armchair next to me. "Are you the police?"

"No, like I said on the phone, I'm working alongside them." I doubted Leo Riley would agree with that statement, but hey-ho. "I believe you jumped with your husband that day?"

"Yes." She picked up a framed photograph from the sideboard next to the chair. "We regularly jumped together." She handed me the photo.

In the picture, a much happier Lesley Thomas was standing next to a bald-headed man. They were wearing matching navy blue jumpsuits.

"The police think your husband may have blacked out? Had he been ill?"

"No. Dale was perfectly well, but I can't think of any other explanation. It seems he never pulled the cord."

"Was he okay otherwise? Was anything troubling him?"

"He was perfectly happy. It wasn't suicide, if that's what you're insinuating!" Her sorrow was suddenly replaced by anger.

"No. Of course not. What about your relationship?"

"What about it? We were perfectly happy, and had been for twelve years."

"You know Alan Carver, I believe?"

"He was one of Dale's best friends."

"Alan suggested that you and Dale might have been having a few—err—issues?"

Her face flushed red. "How dare he! I never did like that man, but I put up with him for Dale's sake. There were no *issues* with our marriage. Alan is recently divorced. Did you know that?"

"I didn't."

"His wife cheated on him, and I can't say I blame her. That seems to have coloured his judgement. He no longer believes it's possible to be happily married. Sad really."

"What about your stepson, Shane? Were Dale and he close?"

"Shane is a waste of space. I knew that the first time I met him, but Dale wouldn't have a bad word said against him. At least, not at first."

"That changed?"

"Even Dale eventually saw through him. Shane came to him for money to finance some half-baked business venture. Dale could see it was destined to fail, so he turned him down. They haven't spoken since. Still, it looks like Shane will get his money now."

"He stands to inherit?"

"Even though they'd fallen out, Dale wouldn't remove Shane from his Will. Everything except this house and the business will be split fifty-fifty between him and me."

"I understand that you didn't normally jump with Skydiving Adventures?"

"No. We usually jump from Robert Lane's plane."

"That's Dale's business partner?"

"Yes, and a close family friend. His plane was in for repairs. We weren't going to bother at all, but Dale suggested we book a ride with Skydiving Adventures. If only we'd stayed at home—" She began to cry.

Lesley Thomas did appear to be devastated by her husband's death—hardly surprising, given the circumstances. She'd had to watch, helpless, as he had plummeted to his death. I couldn't begin to imagine what she must have gone through, as she drifted slowly down to earth—knowing what waited for her on the ground. Just the thought of it sent a shiver down my spine.

One thing was clear, she was not a fan of Alan Carver. I hadn't been aware of his recent divorce. Could that have tainted his views on the Thomas's marriage? Possibly, but I thought I was a pretty good judge of character, and I still believed that Carver was genuinely concerned that his friend's death may have been the result of foul play.

***

My phone rang, but I didn't recognise the number.

"Jill Gooder speaking."

"Jill, it's Susan Bestwick."

Oh bum!

"Hi, Susan."

"I just wanted to ask what you thought of the sculpture?"

"The sculpture? I—err—I."

"Didn't you like it?"

"No, I mean yes, I loved it."

"Thank goodness. I thought you were going to say you hated it."

"Not at all. It was very lifelike."

"Was?"

"I meant 'is'. There's just one thing I wanted to ask you."

"Yes?"

"Well, it's just that — err — well — err."

"Are you sure you're alright, Jill?"

"Fine, yeah. When I came for the sitting, I was — err — I had my clothes on. But when I — got the err — "

"Oh, yes. Sorry. I should have mentioned that I only do sculptures of the naked body. I pride myself on being able to recreate a model's body accurately, even without actually seeing it. I seem to have a kind of x-ray vision."

"I see."

"Did I get it wrong? Too big? Too small? Too perky? Not perky enough?"

"No, they — err — it was fine. Just the right amount of perkyness. Thanks."

"Phew. Thank goodness. It's important to me that you like it."

"Oh, I do. Thanks."

"Where is it?"

"What?"

"The sculpture?"

"Oh, it has pride of place on the mantelpiece."

"Great. Look, I normally take a photo of all the pieces I produce, but because I was in such a hurry, I totally forgot. Could I pop over to your house? Just to take a quick photo?"

"Pop over? Err — sure. But it might be difficult for a couple of days because we're going away."

"Okay, I'll ring you in a few days' time to arrange something. Thanks, Jill. Bye."

"Bye."

Oh bum squared!

Chapter 7

Jules was in the office, knitting.

"Afternoon, Jill."

"Hi. Anything to report?"

"Brent from I-Sweat popped around earlier to see you. He said he'd try again later."

"He's probably going to try to persuade me to sign up for membership."

"You should join, Jill. I feel much better for my new exercise regime."

"I might." Or I might just stick with the custard creams. "How's Gilbert? Still acting strangely?"

"Yeah. I don't know what's wrong with him. Why do men have to be so complicated?"

"I've no idea, but if you ever work it out, let me know, would you? How is his complexion? Has the acne made a comeback?"

"No. His skin is flawless. I wish mine was as good."

As soon as I walked through to my office, Winky pointed to a huge bouquet of flowers on my desk. "Those are for you."

"Okay, now I know you're up to something."

"What do you mean?"

"First you buy me a cake, and—"

"Bake! I *baked* you a cake."

"Okay. First you bake me a cake, and now you buy me flowers. What's going on?"

"Nothing. I felt bad because I persuaded you to give your flowers to Peggy, so, I thought I'd buy you these. Do you like them?"

"They're very nice."

"Smell them."

"Lovely, yes, but I'm still waiting for the other shoe to drop."

"Why are you talking about shoes?"

"It's a saying."

"You two-leggeds have some weird sayings."

"I suppose that you felines have better ones?"

"Of course. Would you like to hear one?"

"Probably not."

"A whisker is never to be sneezed at."

"That doesn't make any sense."

"But a shoe dropping does?"

"Go on, then. I'll bite. What does it mean? The whisker sneeze thing?"

"Isn't it obvious? It means that even when everything seems lost, you should never give up."

"No, it doesn't. You've just made that up."

He shrugged, and then jumped onto the sofa.

Now I felt bad. Perhaps he was genuinely trying to be nice. "Thanks for the flowers."

He was still sulking when I took them through to the outer office.

"Jules, can you put these in water, please?"

"They're beautiful. Who bought those for you?"

"Wink—err—Winkard. An old school friend."

"Called Winkard?"

"Yes. Unusual name, isn't it? Wendy Winkard. Nice woman."

***

Thirty minutes later, I heard the outer door open, and shortly afterwards, Jules popped her head around my door.

"Is it Brent?" I said.

"No, actually it's your accountant, Mr Stone. He wondered if you could spare him a moment."

"Of course. Send him through."

Luther smouldered his way into my office. "Nice flowers. From an admirer?"

"An old school friend, actually."

Winky one-eye-glared at me.

"I was passing by so I thought I'd just pop in to say that Maria and I both enjoyed dinner the other night."

"So did we."

"I must give Jack a call to arrange a game of bowling sometime."

"Yeah. Just don't beat him. He's a terrible loser."

"Really?"

"No, I'm only kidding. Unless it's against me. He hates it when I win."

"What did you think of Maria?"

"She seems very nice." For a bloodsucking vampire.

"She isn't usually so quiet, but she was on edge waiting for the phone call from the hospital."

"She seemed to brighten up once she'd heard from them."

"Yeah, she did."

"Do you two see each other often?"

"Most days." He hesitated. "Jill, do you think it's strange that I don't know where Maria lives?"

"Err—I—err"

"We've been seeing quite a lot of each other, and

usually end up back at my apartment. Don't get me wrong, I'm happy to be with her anywhere, but she has never invited me to her place."

"Maybe it's a mess. Women can be quite untidy. Not me, obviously, but some can. Or maybe she lives in a flat-share, and has noisy flatmates."

"I guess so, but I don't even know whereabouts in Washbridge she lives. Whenever I've offered to drive her home, or to get her a taxi, she always comes up with some excuse why I shouldn't. It's almost as though she doesn't want me to know where she lives. You don't think she has someone else, do you?"

"No, I'm sure that's not it. She'll tell you when she's ready."

"Yeah." He managed a smile. "I guess I'm just impatient. Thanks, Jill. Tell Jack I'll call him to arrange a game, will you?"

"Sure."

After Luther had left, I reflected on what he'd said about Maria. It was obvious she was still living in Candlefield, but she could hardly tell him that. If their relationship was going to progress, she'd have to find herself a base in the human world.

***

I was in my office, talking to Jules, when Brent came in.

"Jill, I was hoping to catch you." He glanced across at the vase of flowers. "From an admirer?"

"They're from an old school friend," I said. "Wendy Winkman."

"I thought you said her name was Winkard?" Jules said.

"That's right Winkard. Her nickname was Winkman."

It was difficult to say who looked more confused: Brent or Jules.

"Thanks, Jules, that will be all." I waited until she'd left my office. "If it's about the subscription, Brent, I'm still thinking about it."

"No. It's not that. I may need your professional services."

"Oh? In that case, take a seat, and tell me what's on your mind."

"George and I are worried that some of our members may be using the club for illegal activities."

"What are they up to?"

"That's just it. We can't be sure that they're up to anything."

"But your suspicionometer is in the red zone?"

"My what?"

"You suspect they may be up to no good?"

"Yeah. We think they might be dealing steroids."

"Have you actually seen any change hands?"

"No. If we had, we could act. We'd cancel their membership, and ban them for life. But we can't get close enough to be sure. That's where you come in."

"You want me to go undercover?"

"Yeah. You look like you need to work out. No one would give you a second glance."

Just what every woman wants to hear.

"The thing is, Jill. The business is still very new, and cashflow isn't great right now."

"Is this leading up to the part where you say you can't pay me?"

"I thought maybe we could come to some kind of

arrangement?"

"What did you have in mind?"

"If you do this, we could give you a free lifetime membership."

"Lifetime? Hmmm, okay then. You'd better tell me everything you know about these people."

***

I'd no sooner pulled onto my drive than Jen arrived home. She was married to Blake, a wizard; they lived across the road from us. Blake had made the brave, but potentially dangerous decision to reveal to his wife that he was a wizard. In some ways, I envied him. It would have been great to be totally open with Jack. But, for me at least, the risk was simply too great.

I was worried for Blake because Jen had been known to speak out of turn. I couldn't help but feel it was only a matter of time before she said the wrong thing to the wrong person. If she did, Blake would be transported back to Candlefield.

"Hi, Jill." She was on her way over.

"Long time no see. How are things?"

"I'm not having the best of days." She frowned. "The stupid washing machine leaked all over the kitchen floor this morning."

"Oh dear. Have you had it long?"

"No. That's what makes it worse. It's brand new; we only got it a week ago."

"The same thing happened to my sister. Hers was an Elf."

"Same as ours. It sounds like there must be a general

fault. Anyway, they're meant to be sending someone around tonight. He's going to get both barrels."

"How is Blake?"

"He's in my bad books. He was the one who suggested we get the new washing machine. There was nothing wrong with the old one. It worked like magic." She flinched. "Not like real magic, obviously. It wasn't a magic washing machine. There's no such thing as a magic washing machine. Or any other magic for that matter."

Give Jen a spade, and she just keeps on digging that hole.

"I hope you get it sorted. Say 'hi' to Blake for me."

"I will. And if you see him, you won't mention the magic washing machine thing, will you?"

"No, Jen. I promise that the word 'magic' will not pass my lips."

***

I was just about to open the door when I heard a noise. There was someone already in the house! Then, I realised what the sound was. It was the vacuum cleaner. Of course! Jack had mentioned that our new cleaner would be coming over to do the initial clean today.

I wasn't sure I dared go inside. I'd never be able to keep a straight face if she introduced herself. Why couldn't Jack have found someone with a sensible name?

Oh well, I couldn't stand there all night. I'd just have to do my best not to fall around laughing. Deep breath, Jill.

What on earth was going on? The noise from the vacuum cleaner seemed to be coming from upstairs, but there were also noises coming from the kitchen—it sounded like someone was mopping the floor. But what really bothered me was the sound of the TV, coming from the lounge.

When I pushed open the door, the sight that greeted me left me speechless.

But not for long.

"Who are you?" I asked the elderly witch who was lying on the sofa. She was eating chocolates, and there was a glass of wine on the coffee table.

"Hello." She muted the TV. "You must be Jill."

"Yes, I am, but who are you?"

"Agatha Crustie. I'm your new cleaner."

I'd expected to laugh when she introduced herself, but this was no laughing matter.

"Why are you eating my chocolates and drinking my wine?"

"I couldn't find the whiskey."

"Why aren't you cleaning the house?"

"I am. Can't you hear the vacuum and the mop?"

"You're using magic to clean my house?"

"Of course. You wouldn't expect me to do it, would you? With my old bones?"

"If I'd wanted it cleaned by magic, I could have done it myself."

"That's what I said to Mirabel. I asked her why you didn't do that. She said you were a strange one."

"You know my grandmother?"

"Of course, dear. She was the one who put me onto the job in the first place."

"I'm sorry, but I don't think this is going to work out."

Her face fell, and she looked on the verge of tears. "You were my last hope. I've been rather down on my luck lately. If I don't bring in some money soon, I'll be thrown out of the house. Me and Jeb."

"Is Jeb your husband?"

"No. He's my boa constrictor. I never had kids. Jeb is my little boy."

Little? A boa constrictor?

"I suppose I'd better clear my things away." She started for the door.

"Wait! Maybe we could give it a trial?"

"Really? Your grandmother said you were a little darling."

"I thought she said I was 'a strange one'?"

"She was only joking."

"You can't do any magic when Jack is around."

"Of course. You can rely on Crustie."

"And no more wine. Or chocolates."

Chapter 8

The next morning, Jack was up before me, which was quite remarkable considering he still hadn't got home when I'd gone to bed the previous night.

"I thought you'd have a lie in this morning." I yawned.

"Couldn't sleep."

"Why were you so late last night?"

"We had a hostage situation."

"What happened?"

"Just a domestic gone wrong. No one got hurt, thank goodness. It looked like it might get nasty for a while. The good news is that I've got this afternoon off."

"How come?"

"I'm owed half a day, apparently. Do you fancy meeting up? We could check out that new mall."

"I'm not sure I'll be able to get away. I've got a lot on at the moment."

"Surely you could spare a few hours?"

"I guess so. It's that 'Big' day promotion at Coffee Triangle today. We could check that out first."

"What's going on there?"

"No idea. It's all very mysterious."

"Okay. Will you give me a call later to confirm?"

"Sure."

"I see *my* new cleaner did an excellent job yesterday." He sounded very smug.

"Not bad."

"Come on, Jill, admit it. My Mrs Crustie is better than your Mrs Mopp."

"Okay. Your Mrs Crustie is magic. Happy now?

***

Mr Ivers was in the toll booth.

"Morning, Jill." He seemed to be standing awkwardly, with his chest puffed out.

"I thought you were going to be working in the office?"

"Slight change of plan. I'll be on duty here one or two days each week."

Goody gumdrops.

"Have you noticed anything different about me, Jill?"

"Have you got a bad leg? You seem to be standing rather awkwardly."

He pushed his chest even further out. That's when I spotted it.

"What's that on your jacket? Is it some kind of medal?"

"Oh, this little thing? I'm surprised you noticed it. It's kind of embarrassing. I don't like to talk about it."

"Okay." I held out the toll fee.

"But seeing as you asked. I was awarded this for exceptional bravery in the course of my duties."

"I'm very impressed. What did you do? Did someone fall in the river? Did you dive in and rescue them?"

"No, nothing like that. I can't swim. It was the tiger. The company felt my actions deserved recognition."

Huh? Unless my memory was playing tricks on me, Mr Ivers' actions comprised of locking himself in the toll booth, and screaming like a little girl.

"Would you like a selfie with me?" He offered.

"Thanks, but I'm in a bit of a rush. Why don't you ask Jack when he comes by? I'm sure he'll be up for it."

Snigger.

Mrs V was behind her desk, knitting. Or at least, the needles in her hand were clicking away, but there was no wool in sight.

"Wi-Fi Needles, Mrs V?"

"Yes, dear. Dotty Forelock, a friend from the knitting circle, has gone down with a bad case of flu. She needed to get a cardigan finished for her new baby granddaughter. I said I'd lend a hand."

"So, the cardigan is actually at Dotty's house?"

"That's right, dear. Dotty is in bed. The cardigan is on the bedside cabinet so she can keep an eye on progress."

"Isn't it difficult? Knitting something you can't see?"

She smiled. "Not when you've been doing it as long as I have. I often knit in the dark to save on electricity."

"This is for you." Winky handed me a giant custard cream-shaped tin. "I know they're your favourites."

Now I was really worried. Whatever he was up to had to be very bad for him to give me a cake, flowers and now a giant tin of custard creams.

"You're scaring me, Winky. What have you done?"

"Nothing. I just figured it was time to show my appreciation for everything you do for me."

"Is it really bad?"

"Is what really bad?"

"Whatever it is that you've done that means you have to give me a cake, flowers and custard creams to compensate."

"Are you as suspicious of Jack when he buys you a present?"

I laughed. "The next time he buys me a present will be the first."

"Well, that's the difference between him and me. I know how to look after the ladies in my life. You should bring him in here. I'll have a word with him."

"He's a human. Have you forgotten?"

"Oh yeah. Well, there's your answer. They're a tight-fisted lot, humans, all of them. Why do you think I chose to live with you?"

"I assumed it was because you thought I looked kind."

"Nah. I figured you'd keep me in the style to which I wanted to become accustomed. Which is why I'm showing my appreciation. Do you believe me now?"

"I suppose so."

"Good. Let's get busy with the salmon and cream, then."

I'd no sooner given Winky his food than my phone rang.

"Aunt Lucy?"

"Jill, I've just had a message from Imelda Barrowtop's daughter. She wants you to attend the reading of Imelda's Will. It's in a few days' time."

"Me? I didn't know Imelda. The first time I met her was on her deathbed."

"I know. That's exactly what I said to Petunia, but she insisted it was important that you attended."

"What time is it? And where?"

"I'm not sure. She said she'd let me have the details later. When she calls back, shall I tell her you'll be there?"

"I guess so."

"Okay. Thanks, Jill."

Why on earth did I need to be at the reading of Imelda Barrowtop's Will?

I'd find out soon enough.

* * *

The police seemed to have accepted that Dale Thomas's death had been an accident or possibly suicide. I could only assume that they were basing that conclusion on information given to them by the accident investigator and medical examiner. Before I accepted that theory, I wanted to speak to both of those people myself.

One slight problem: why would they talk to me?

Answer: they wouldn't.

But they *would* speak to Leo Riley. So, much as the thought appalled me, I was going to have to use magic to give myself the appearance of my favourite detective. I already had the details of the two experts in question—I'd obtained them courtesy of a quick 'invisible' visit to Washbridge police station.

* * *

I felt dirty. I'd just cast the 'doppelganger' spell to transform myself into that loathsome man.

"Detective Riley?" Arnold Besafe, the accident investigator, was apparently on a break when I called at his office. "Can I get you a coffee?"

"No, thanks. I'd just like to double-check some details on the Thomas case."

"The skydiver? Didn't you get my report?"

"I did, and excellent work it was too."

"Thank you." He blushed.

Flattery always did the trick—he was mine for the taking now.

"From your report, I take it there's no doubt that the parachute was in good working order?"

"None at all. Most of the time when I get called in on cases like this, the opposite is true. It's invariably a faulty parachute that's to blame, but not this time. If the deceased had pulled the cord, it would have deployed."

"There's no doubt in your mind about that?"

"None."

"So, that leaves us with only two possibilities: suicide or some kind of blackout?"

"No. There is a third which I mentioned in my report."

"Remind me."

"It's possible the deceased was unconscious when he left the aeroplane."

"You mean that someone could have knocked him out, and then pushed him out of the aeroplane?"

"Exactly. Although, as I said in my report, that is the least likely explanation."

"Right. Thank you for your time Mr Besafe."

"My pleasure, Detective Riley."

Hmm? That was food for thought. Was it possible that Dale Thomas had been knocked out by someone in the aeroplane? As far as I was aware there were only two other people aboard that plane: the pilot, Gerry Southland, and Thomas's wife.

Next, I paid a visit to the medical examiner.

"Leo? I wasn't expecting to see you. You're not

cancelling tonight, are you? I've bought new lingerie, specially."

Whoops! It seemed that medical examiner, Sheila Treetop, and Leo Riley had much more than just a professional relationship. That was going to make things ten times more difficult.

"Of course not, Sheila."

"Sheila? Since when did I become Sheila again? I thought I was your little 'Tops'?" She ran a finger across my lips. Oh dear, this wasn't going at all as I'd hoped.

"Sorry. Of course you're still my little 'Tops'." Where was a vomit bag when you needed one? "I'm just a little stressed this morning."

"I can help with that."

Oh bum!

I took a couple of steps back — out of reach. "As tempted as I am, Tops, I'm due in a meeting in ten minutes."

"That's plenty of time."

"No, seriously, Tops. I have to get back."

She sighed, and didn't try to hide her disappointment. "What is it you need from me, then?"

"Just a quick recap on the Thomas case."

"The skydiver? What's to tell? It's all there in my report."

"I know, but I just want to be sure. Can you sum it up for me in a few words?"

She sighed again. "No pre-existing medical conditions."

"Suicide then?"

"That's not what my report said. Did you even read it, Leo?"

"I only had time to skim it."

"It could be suicide or he could have blacked out.

There's no way of knowing."

"But you said there was no pre-existing medical condition?"

"People black out all the time."

"Of course. Could someone have knocked him out, and then pushed him out of the aeroplane?"

"The injuries sustained from the fall made it impossible to tell if he'd been struck in the aeroplane. It's possible, but unlikely, in my opinion."

"So, your money would be on—?"

"A blackout or suicide."

"Thanks." I started for the door.

"Is that it? Not even a kiss?"

"Err—later—I promise."

I made a dash for it.

Leo Riley would have a lot of explaining to do on their date.

Snigger.

That had been a lot more difficult than I'd expected, but at least I was clear in my mind on one thing now: there were three possible causes of death, and one of those was murder.

***

I was still feeling incredibly guilty over Barry. It had been a mistake to take him to the human world, and I wanted to make sure he was okay.

"Where's Barry, Aunt Lucy?"

"Fast asleep upstairs. We were at the park for almost two hours. Dolly was there with Babs. The two dogs ran each other ragged. I thought I was going to have to carry him back home."

"I'm sorry about dropping him back on you like this."

"Don't be daft. I love the big soft thing. This house seemed empty when he was in the human world. What about Jack? How did he take it?"

"He's okay. He realised it had been a mistake."

"I'm glad you popped in, Jill. I was going to give you a call."

"Oh?"

"That horrible woman from the TV had one of her minions drop this off for you." Aunt Lucy handed me an envelope.

I knew what it was even before I opened it.

"Bad news?" Aunt Lucy looked concerned.

"It's the list of questions she wants to ask me in the interview."

"Are you still going to do it?"

"I don't see I have any choice. I promised I would, and if I go back on my word, she's only going to pursue me around Candlefield. Probably best to get it over with."

"When is it?"

"No date as yet. She wants me to call her to arrange something."

Chapter 9

Oh bum! I'd promised to meet Jack at Coffee Triangle at two o' clock, and it was now almost twenty past.

"You're late." He looked decidedly unimpressed.

"I thought we said twenty-five past."

"Why would we arrange to meet at twenty-five past?"

"I must have misheard you, sorry. Have you found out what the 'Big' day is all about?"

"No clue. Let's go in and see."

The promotion, whatever it was, had clearly had the desired effect because the place was chock-a-block. Normally, if it had been that busy, I would have turned around and left, but I wanted to know what the 'Big' day was all about.

By the time we'd fought our way to the counter, I had my answer.

"Giant instruments?" I groaned. "Is that it?"

"I think it's a clever idea." Clearly, Jack was easily impressed.

There were a number of the over-sized instruments scattered around the shop. To my right was an enormous tambourine, which was almost as tall as Jack. Off to the left was a man-size pair of maracas. As an additional part of the celebrations, the management had dispensed with the usual tradition of having a single instrument theme for the day. Instead, customers could have the choice of any of the percussion instruments on offer. The resultant din was almost unbearable, as people banged drums, struck gongs, and shook tambourines.

"What do you want?" Jack asked.

"A caramel latte and a blueberry muffin, please."

"I know that. I meant which instrument."

"I don't care."

"A triangle?"

"Anything but a triangle." I hadn't mentioned my irrational fear of the three-sided percussion instrument to Jack.

"There you go." He passed me a tambourine. He had chosen a drum—typical man! "Over there!" He pointed. "There's a free table."

When I reached the table, I stopped dead in my tracks.

"What's wrong?" Jack almost crashed into the back of me.

"Let's find another table."

"There aren't any others. What's wrong with this one?"

Jack stepped around me and took a seat.

"I think I'll stand."

"Don't be silly. Come and sit next to the giant triangle."

That was the problem. There was a freaking giant triangle leaning against the table.

"I'm okay here." I couldn't take my eyes off the three-sided monster.

"Please yourself. This giant triangle is great, isn't it?" He banged on the drum.

"If you like that kind of thing." I gave an involuntary shiver.

"Wait a minute." He grinned. "Are you scared of triangles?"

"Don't be ridiculous." I forced a laugh. "Come on, drink up. It's too busy in here. Let's go to the mall."

I didn't wait for him. I just hightailed it out of there, and away from that freaky giant triangle.

"What was that all about, back there?" Jack asked, as we

made our way to the mall.

"It was too crowded."

"You didn't even eat your muffin. I've never known you to leave a muffin before."

Drat! I'd been so freaked out that I'd forgotten to pick it up. I could always dash back for it. But no—it was too risky. The giant triangle was probably lying in wait.

What do you mean, I need serious help?

The mall wasn't quite as busy as it had been on opening day, but it was still mighty crowded.

"What did you think of 'Central Shark'?" I grinned.

"Of what?"

"Come on, Jack. This place is called The Central."

"I know that."

"So, the shark must be 'Central Shark'."

"What shark?"

"The giant one above the entrance that we just walked through."

"I didn't see it."

Give me strength.

"Look over there." Jack pointed. "A trampoline."

"You are not getting me on a trampoline."

"It isn't for visitors. There's a demonstration by the Washbridge Flyers at three o' clock. We should definitely watch that."

"Watch people bouncing up and down? That'll be exciting."

"Trampolining is a serious sport."

"Of course it isn't. You'll be telling me next that jumping up and down on a bouncy castle is a sport too."

"I'd like to see the Washbridge Flyers."

"Okay." Yawn. Hopefully, he'd have forgotten about it by three o' clock, so we could do something more exciting. Like watching paint dry.

"Jill!" a female voice called.

It took me a moment to place her, but then I realised it was Brenda from The Coven, the superstar singing combo who had once tried to recruit me to be the 'The'.

What do you mean you're confused? You should have read all of the books.

"Hi, Brenda. Long time, no see. This is Jack."

"I'm a big fan of The Coven." He fawned. The man was such a creep.

"Actually, I'm no longer with The Coven."

"Really?" I said. "How come? I thought they'd been killing it?"

"They have, and I'm sure they'll continue to without me. I started off as a solo singer, and that's my real passion, so I decided to go on my own again. It's a bit scary though."

"I'm sure you'll do great." Jack gushed.

"Thanks. I hope so. My first show is at Washbridge Arena in a couple of weeks." She took a flyer out of her handbag, and handed it to me.

"I don't get it. I thought you said you were going solo?"

"I am."

"But this says 'We' in concert?"

"That's right. Do you remember The Coven's closing number?"

"Who could forget it?"

"In that finale, I always used to be the 'We' in the 'We Are The Coven' routine. No one knows me as Brenda.

Everyone knows me as 'We'. Do you see?"

"Yes." Clear as mud.

"I hope you and Jack will come and see me."

"I wouldn't miss it for the world." Jack was still gushing.

"Okay. Well, I'd better get off," Brenda said. "I need to buy some new outfits for the show. Nice to see you again, Jill. Nice to meet you, Jack."

"We should definitely go," Jack said, after she'd left.

"To see 'We'? I don't think so. You should give Kathy a call. Her music taste is on a par with yours."

Suddenly, there was an ear-piercing scream, which caused everyone to stop dead in their tracks. The whole mall came to a halt and fell silent, as everyone looked at the man standing by the rails on the floor above. A few feet away from him, a hysterical woman was screaming.

"I'll drop her!" The man shouted.

'Her' was the baby girl he was holding out over the rails.

"Please, Mike. Put her down!" The woman was weeping.

"If I can't be with you, what's the point?"

A number of security men had appeared, but none of them dared make a move towards the man for fear that he would drop the child.

"Don't do anything stupid," one of the security men shouted.

"Shut your mouth. This has nothing to do with you. Come any closer, and I'll drop her."

I glanced at the trampoline. It was a few feet short of being directly under the man. If he carried out his threat, and dropped the child, she would hit the tiled floor.

"I said stay back!" the man shouted. He'd seen one of the security men move a few feet closer.

The screams were deafening. Whether deliberately or by accident, the man had let the baby fall. I had only a split second to act. I cast the 'move' spell, and pushed the trampoline a couple of feet to the right.

It was enough. The baby hit the trampoline, and bounced back into the air. A woman, one of the Washbridge Flyers, leapt onto the trampoline and grabbed the baby. You could have heard a pin drop as everyone waited.

"She's okay!" The woman declared to loud cheers. The baby's mother was already rushing down the steps. The baby's father had been tackled to the ground by a number of security guards.

"Thank goodness she's alright." Jack squeezed my hand. "I thought she was dead for sure. I didn't think the trampoline was in the right place to catch her."

Fortunately, everyone had been so busy watching the baby that they hadn't noticed the trampoline slide across the floor.

It was at times like this that I gave thanks that I had magical powers.

"Can we go now?" My feet were killing me. We'd been at the mall for almost three hours.

"Okay, but we'll definitely have to come back again when we have more time."

More time? Just how long did he want to spend there?

"I had no idea that there'd be a branch of 'Bowled Over' here," Jack said.

"Neither did I." Or I wouldn't have come.

Jack had been beside himself with excitement when he'd realised that there was a ten-pin bowling store in the mall. I hadn't spotted it on my first visit, otherwise I would have made sure we'd given it a wide berth.

"Do you think I picked the right shirt?" he asked.

"It took you almost two hours to decide, so I would hope so."

"It took me ten minutes, max."

"It felt like two hours."

"You don't think the green one might have been better? I could always go back and swap it?"

"No. The blue one is fine."

"I bought a red one."

"That's what I meant. The red one suits you."

"I might treat myself to a new ball, the next time I come."

"If you decide to, do me a favour, would you?"

"What?"

"Take Trevor or Luther with you. If I have to come, I'll be comatose by the time you've picked one."

"I will. At least that way I won't have to listen to you complaining all the time. Or were you 'commenting' again? Anyway, where's this shark you've been going on about?" '

***

Mrs Rollo came out to meet us when we pulled onto the drive.

"Jack, Jill, I've made a cake to celebrate Marco's visit. I have a couple of slices for the two of you."

"Thanks ever so much, Mrs Rollo." Jack took them from her.

The man was an accomplished actor. He actually sounded pleased to receive the cake, which would no doubt go in our bin as soon as we got inside the house.

"It's such a pity that Barry had to go back." Mrs Rollo looked quite sad.

"I agree," I said. "But Jack just couldn't get along with him."

Mrs Rollo glared at Jack.

"That's not entirely true, is it, Jill?" Jack sounded miffed. "We both agreed that he'd be better off in a bigger house where there'd be someone with him all day."

"I know, but I still miss him." I sighed.

Jack shot me a look.

"Oh, yes, I almost forgot," Mrs Rollo said. "I managed to get a couple of tickets for you for the talk that Marco is giving at Paranormal Activity Watch." She produced them from her pocket.

"I'm sorry, Mrs Rollo," I said. "It's not really our —"

"We'd love to go." Jack took them from her. "It sounds really interesting, doesn't it, Jill?"

"Does it? Yeah, I guess."

"Okay, well I'd better get back inside. I have some cupcakes in the oven. I'll make sure to save you some."

Oh goody.

"What were you thinking, taking those tickets?" I said, once we were back in the house.

"It could be interesting." He dropped the slices of cake into the bin. "And what's with blaming me for sending Barry back?"

"It was your idea to get shot of him."

"I miss the big lump."

"You liar."

"Anyhow, this talk could be interesting. Don't you find the whole idea of paranormal beings fascinating?"

"Not really. It's all just fairy tales."

"How can you possibly know that? They could be living among us right now, and we'd never know. Maybe I'm actually a wizard."

"I know for sure that's not true."

"How?"

"Wizards have a much better taste in shirts."

Chapter 10

I left the house early the next morning because I wanted to take a closer look at Magical Skincare to find out what was happening with Gilbert. This time though, I needed to get a look inside the building.

I hid across the road from the unit, and when I spotted Gilbert arriving, I cast the 'invisible' spell. I followed him to the door, and slipped in unseen behind him. I'd expected to find a sales office and some kind of production line. In fact, all of the rooms except the largest one were empty.

In the centre of that room was a large cauldron. Standing around it, were three witches, dressed in formal robes just like the one I'd worn at the Levels Competition. The tallest of the three had a wart on her nose that was even bigger than Grandma's. The witch standing next to her had the most enormous feet I'd ever seen. The last of the three was tiny and only came up to the waist of the other two.

Gilbert was standing with the young man and woman who'd been working with him at the mall. Once again, all three of them had terrible acne.

"Time for your dip," The Wart cackled.

"Caps on!" Giant Feet yelled.

Gilbert and his two companions picked up what looked like swimming caps, and pulled them onto their heads to cover their hair.

"Harnesses on!" Tiny Witch shouted.

The three young people fastened themselves into harnesses, and then clipped a cord to some kind of conveyor belt which was running above their heads.

"Dip them!" The Wart ordered.

Giant Feet threw the switch, and immediately Gilbert and his co-workers were hoisted into the air and then flipped upside down. The conveyor belt then began to move slowly towards the centre of the room. Gilbert was the first in line. When he was immediately above the cauldron, he was lowered so that his head was fully submerged in the dark green, gooey liquid. After no more than a few seconds, he was hoisted back up. The same thing happened to the other two.

The three of them were lowered to the ground and released from their harnesses. After removing the 'swimming caps', they wiped the remaining goo from their faces, which were now blemish free.

"All done, Madam Frumaker," Giant Feet addressed The Wart.

"Excellent," The Wart said. "Off you go then."

The three young people made their way out of the building. I followed them.

What had I just witnessed? When Gilbert and his two colleagues had arrived, they'd had terrible acne, but after being dipped into the gooey substance, they had perfect skin. Did they do that every day? It certainly looked that way.

This had confirmed my suspicions that Magical Skincare was a front for some kind of magic potion, but why go to all the trouble of dipping the young people in the cauldron? Why not just apply the ointment they were trying to sell at the mall? Before I took this any further I needed some advice, and much as it pained me to admit it, the best person to give me that advice would be

Grandma.

***

Dale Thomas's son, Shane, had agreed to see me. He was living in a flat-share in a run-down block of flats in the seedier part of Washbridge.

"What d'ya want?" A young woman, with a pierced nose, answered the door. She blew and then burst a gum bubble. "Are you from the social?"

"No. My name is Jill Gooder. Shane Thomas is expecting me."

"Shane? You sure? No one ever visits Shane."

"I'm sure. Would you tell him I'm here?"

"You'd better come in. Got any ciggies?"

"I don't smoke."

"Shane!" she yelled at the top of her voice. "Some woman here to see you."

"Who?" A young man wearing torn jeans and no shirt, appeared in a doorway.

"Jill Gooder. I rang yesterday."

"Oh yeah. You'd better come through."

I followed him into what I assumed was a bedroom, although it was difficult to be sure. Somewhere under all that rubbish, a bed may have been lurking. Shane put on a t-shirt that looked like it hadn't seen the inside of a washing machine for several weeks.

"Like I said on the phone." He lit a cigarette. "I don't understand what it is you're investigating. Dad never pulled the cord. That's what I heard."

"That's right."

"Must have been an accident then. Blacked out or

something."

"Probably."

"It wasn't suicide, if that's what you're thinking. Dad would never have topped himself."

"Do you skydive?"

He laughed. "Me? Not likely. Dad tried to get me to go with him when I was younger, but I didn't want to know."

"I heard you and your father didn't have a particularly good relationship?"

"Who said that? I bet it was Lesley?"

"Did you?"

"Not particularly. We used to be okay before he married that witch."

"I take it you don't get along with your stepmother?"

"That would be an understatement. She never liked me from the get-go, and the feeling is mutual. She never loved my dad."

"What makes you say that?"

"It was obvious to anyone." He snorted. "Except Dad. He was besotted."

"I understand you went to your father with a business idea."

"I did. A good one it was too, but he just pooh-poohed it."

"What was it?"

"An online marketplace for bottle tops. And before you laugh, there's big money to be made in bottle tops."

"I believe you."

"Anyway, he turned me down flat."

"That must have made you angry?"

"Course it did, but it doesn't mean I wanted to kill him

if that's what you're thinking."

"When was the last time you saw him?"

"Not sure." He shrugged. "A couple of months ago, I guess."

"Are you going to be long, Shane?" Bubble-gum girl stuck her head around the door. "We're meant to be going to the launderette."

"We're done here, aren't we?"

"We are. Thanks for your time."

Shane Thomas may not have had a good relationship with his father, but I wasn't sure the frustrated bottle top entrepreneur was murderer material. I'd found his remarks about his stepmother interesting though. If it was true that she had never loved Dale Thomas, that could change everything because she stood to benefit from his death, and was one of only two other people in the aeroplane.

I made a call to Gerry Southland.

"Gerry, It's Jill Gooder. I came to see you the other day."

"I remember."

"Is there any possibility that Dale Thomas could have been knocked unconscious, and pushed out of the plane?"

"Is that a joke?" He laughed. "Of course that's not possible. I have a clear view of the jumpers before they leave the plane. They were both fully conscious when they jumped. No one pushed anyone out."

"Okay, Gerry. Sorry to have troubled you."

That seemed to rule out foul play. I was back to just two possible explanations: a blackout or suicide. It was time to call Alan Carver.

"Alan, it's Jill Gooder."

"Have you got something for me?"

"Nothing. That's just it. I don't think there's anything to find. It looks like an accident or, at worst, suicide."

"I still don't buy it."

"These things do happen."

"I know, but something just doesn't feel right about this. Is there anyone else you still have to talk to?"

"Possibly, but I didn't want to run up your bill any further on a wild goose chase."

"Let me worry about the money. I'd like you to see this through to the bitter end."

"If you're sure?"

"Positive."

It was just as well that Luther hadn't overheard that conversation. He would have said I was crazy trying to talk someone into dropping a case, but I hated working on something when I knew that there was nothing to find. But, it was Carver's money, so his call.

***

On my way back to the office, I called in at a print shop. The large sign outside read 'F For Print'.

"Hi, how can I help you?" The man behind the counter had a big red ink smudge on his nose.

"Hi. You've got a — err — on your nose."

"Oh?" He wiped at it, but it made no difference.

"It's still there."

He tried again.

That's when I realised — it wasn't ink; he just had a very

red nose. If Santa ever needed help again, he'd know who to call.

"That's it — all gone. I noticed your sign is damaged."

"Oh?"

"Part of the 'P' must have fallen off. It says 'F for Print' instead of 'P for Print'."

"It's not damaged. It's supposed to be an 'F'. The 'F' stands for Fred. That's me, Fred Hinkman, at your service."

"I see."

"What can I do for you?"

I passed the photograph to Fred, and explained exactly what I was after.

"No problem. I'll give you a call when they're ready."

I was almost back at the office when my phone rang. It was Brent from I-Sweat.

"Jill, you said I should give you a call the next time the suspicious guys were in the gym."

"Are they there now?"

"Yeah. Can you get around here?"

"I'm almost back at the office. I should be with you in a couple of minutes."

"Hi, Jill." Jules was behind the desk.

"Any messages?"

"No. Can I have a word about Gilbert?"

"Not just now, Jules, I have to go straight back out."

I dashed into my office, and picked up my sports bag.

"Hey, hold on!" Winky called after me.

"Can't stop. I'm on a case."

"What about my salmon?"

I hurried past the I-Sweat reception, and into the changing room. When I came out, Brent was waiting for me just inside the gym.

"Over there, in the far corner," he whispered.

"Okay. I'm on it."

It occurred to me that the last time I'd been in there was when Gavin had tried to kill me. If it hadn't been for Winky I would have been a goner. That made me feel guilty for not having given him any salmon before I rushed out.

The four men were all huddled together, talking in low voices. One thing struck me immediately — they were all vampires. Brent had told me he suspected they might be dealing steroids. I wasn't so sure, but the only way to find out was to listen in on their conversation, and to watch if anything was passed between them.

If I got too close, I might arouse their suspicions, so I picked a treadmill a little distance from where they were standing. Trust me to pick one of the new models. It was different to the ones I'd used before. I pressed the button for what I thought was 'jog' mode.

Wham! I shot off the treadmill, and hit the floor with a thud.

"Ouch!"

"Jill, are you okay?" Brent was standing over me.

"What happened?" My elbows and knees had taken most of the impact.

"You switched the speed to max."

"I did?"

"Can you stand up?" He helped me to my feet. The four vampires had disappeared.

"I'm alright. Sorry, Brent, I rather messed that up."

"It's okay. I'm just glad you're not hurt."

"I don't think they're dealing steroids."

"What are they up to, then?"

"I'm not sure yet, but I'll stay on the case until I find out."

I changed, and hobbled back to my office.

"Are you okay, Jill?" Jules sounded concerned.

"Fine. Just a tough workout."

"I'm getting really worried about Gilbert. He's acting stranger and stranger."

"Would you like me to check if there's something going on with him?"

"Would you mind? That would be great."

"Leave it with me."

"What happened to you?" Winky grinned. "You look like you've been run over by a steamroller."

"I've been next door for a workout."

"It obviously did you a power of good. Now about that salmon."

I was still nursing my bruises when Winky lapped up the last of his milk.

"Just what the doctor ordered." He licked his lips, and then jumped onto the sofa. "So, how's Barry?"

"I've taken him back. He was missing the park."

"Who takes a canary to the park?"

Oh bum! I was so distracted by my injuries that I'd totally forgotten I'd told Winky that Barry was a canary.

"He finds the cage a little claustrophobic, so I take him to the park so he can fly around."

"In the park? Doesn't he fly away?"

"I tie a cord to his foot."

"That's cruel."

"It's a very long cord, and it's made of a soft material."

"And you do this in the park?"

"Yeah, like I said."

"Don't you get some strange looks?"

"A few."

Chapter 11

"What do you think of canaries?" I asked Jack over breakfast.

"Canaries? Why?"

"Oh, no reason. I was dreaming about them."

"I'm looking forward to the talk at PAW tonight, aren't you?"

"Not really. You do realise that every nutjob in Washbridge will be there, don't you?"

"You shouldn't be so ready to dismiss things you don't understand. "

"I do not do that! Take your obsession with ugly bowling shirts. I don't understand that at all, but I don't dismiss it."

"Why can't you accept that there may be other creatures living among us?"

"You could be right. Maybe Mrs Rollo is actually an alien. Or Mr Hosey? Come to think of it, I could definitely believe that Mr Hosey is from a different planet. And Mr Ivers."

"I'm not talking about aliens. I mean things like ghosts or werewolves."

I laughed. "You've been watching too many bad movies."

"We'll see. Maybe you'll change your mind after Marco's talk."

Not long after Jack had left for work, Kathy rang.

"Do you and Jack want to come over tonight? We're celebrating."

"Sorry, we can't make it tonight. What's the occasion?"

"Pete has landed the Washbridge House contract."

"That's brilliant. Well done him."

"It was down to your neighbour that he got it."

"Megan? How come?"

"Pete knew he was down to the last two. He was invited to the house to make his case in front of the owner and his son. When he got there, Megan was the other candidate. She obviously hadn't realised she was up against Pete. When it was time for them to make their pitches, Megan said she was withdrawing her bid. She thanked them for the opportunity, but said she didn't feel she had enough experience or sufficient resources to take on the contract. The owner had no choice but to award the contract to Pete."

"Maybe Megan had realised it was too big a job for her to take on?"

"I don't think so. According to Pete, she'd brought lots of material to help with her presentation. She only decided to withdraw when she realised that if she won, Pete would lose out."

"Sounds to me like you may have misjudged her."

"I know. I feel terrible about some of the things I've said and done."

"Like painting over her van?"

"Thanks, Jill. I don't need you to rub it in. I suggested to Pete that we might ask her and her boyfriend out for a meal."

"You're too late. She's dumped him. It turns out that he was dating both her and Mad at the same time."

"The two-timing pig."

"Don't worry. He got his comeuppance."

"If she's single again, maybe the dinner isn't such a

good idea. What else could I do?"

"How about being civil with her? That would be a start."

"You're right. I'm going to be extra nice to her from now on. Anyway, how come you two can't make it tonight? It's not like you ever go anywhere."

"Jack has roped me into going to some stupid talk at PAW."

"What's that? Some kind of animal charity?"

"No. It stands for Paranormal Activity Watch."

She laughed. "You're kidding?"

"I wish I was. Our neighbour's brother is over from Australia. He's the one giving the talk."

"Ghosts and stuff?"

"Yeah. That kind of thing."

"I'm surprised Jack wants to go. He seems too level-headed for that kind of nonsense."

"Don't you believe it. He's dead keen."

"It might be a laugh."

"I doubt it. Anyway, I'd better get going."

"Hang on. I'm meant to remind you about the sponsorship money you owe Mikey."

"I thought it was Jack who had sponsored him?"

"No, it's definitely your name on the form. Twenty-six pounds. Don't make me send the debt-collectors after you."

"Don't worry. I'll let you have it. How's Lizzie doing? The ghost tour was a bit of a damp squib. Has that put her off them?"

"I wish. She's as keen as ever. In fact, just this morning, she asked me to cancel her subscription to Girly Girl comic, and get her one to Spooky Monthly instead."

"Oh, well, I'm sure she'll grow out of it eventually. By the way, I need a word with Grandma. Do you know if she'll be in Ever today?"

"She's probably there already. She told me yesterday that she'd be in early. Something about tweaking the settings on Wi-Fi Needles."

***

"Jill, you made me jump." Grandma sat up on the sun lounger. She was wearing a swimming costume and sunglasses.

"I can see you're busy tweaking settings," I said.

"What are you talking about?"

"Nothing. Do you have a moment?"

"I had hoped to top up my tan before the shop opened. Is it urgent?"

"It might be. Do you know anyone by the name of Madam Frumaker?"

"I know a Dorothy Frumaker."

"Does she have a — err." I touched my finger to my nose. "On her — err — "

"A what on her what?"

Oh bum! "Never mind. How do you know Frumaker?"

"She has something of a reputation in Candlefield." Grandma applied more sun cream. "I'm surprised you haven't heard about her."

"I can't say I have."

"She concocted what was meant to be the ultimate beauty potion. For a short while, it looked as though it might make her fortune."

"What went wrong?"

"It did what it said on the tin. It made people beautiful, but the effects only lasted for twenty-four hours. And then 'bam', I was back to where I was before."

"*You*? You used it?"

"Me? No, of course not. What would I need with a beauty potion? I'm beautiful enough, aren't I?"

"Err — yes, of course. So, it didn't work?"

"Not for any length of time. When word got out, no one would buy it. Come to think of it, I haven't heard anything of Frumaker for some time. Why did you ask about her?"

"It looks as though she's now selling her potion here in the human world. At least, I think she might be, but she's marketing it as acne cream."

"She's got some nerve. I hope it's more effective on acne than it was as a beauty treatment."

"It isn't. It seems to suffer from the same issues. It's only effective for a short period of time."

"How come you know so much about this?"

"My PA's boyfriend is selling the stuff."

"I'd hardly call Annabel's gentleman friend a '*boy*friend'. And anyway, I thought he was a lawyer."

"Not Mrs V. My other PA, Jules. Her boyfriend, Gilbert, is doing promotions for Frumaker's company, Magical Skincare."

"You should tell him to pack it in."

"It's gone beyond that. I took a look inside the industrial unit where she's brewing the stuff. It was horrible. They dipped Gilbert's head into a cauldron full of some awful gooey stuff."

"Oh dear. That isn't good."

"What do you mean?"

"The effectiveness of Frumaker's potion got less and less the more often it was used. It sounds like your PA's boyfriend is so resistant to it now, that he's being dipped into the undiluted potion."

"Are you suggesting the stuff they sell in the bottles has been diluted?"

"By a factor of at least fifty, I'd guess. The potion in that cauldron will be extremely powerful."

"Could it have side effects?"

"I wouldn't be surprised. Why? Has he grown another head?"

"Nothing like that, but he is acting strangely. A bit like a zombie."

"That'll be the potion, and it'll only get worse."

"Thanks, Grandma. I think it's time I paid a visit to Madam Frumaker."

"I'll come with you."

"No, it's okay. I've got this one."

***

Before I could put a stop to Frumaker and her acne potion, I had a funeral to attend. I hadn't been invited to Dale Thomas's funeral, but I figured it might help my investigation if I could see all the interested parties in one place. I planned to make myself invisible. That way, I should be able to get close enough to listen in on the conversations of the mourners.

I didn't bother to attend the church service. Instead, I waited by the side of the open grave. There was a bigger turnout than I'd expected — a mix of friends, relatives and work colleagues. Lesley Thomas was front and centre at the graveside. She was being comforted by a woman, whose facial features suggested she was probably Lesley's sister. Dale's son, Shane, was there too, but he was standing some distance from his stepmother. There was no sign of Shane's bubble-gum blowing friend. Alan Carver was standing next to Shane. Robert Lane, who I recognised from the photograph I'd seen, was standing next to a woman who I took to be his wife. Although they didn't actually speak, it was obvious from their body language that there was some kind of tension between them — as though they'd had an argument earlier.

"You?" Lesley Thomas spat the word.

I followed her gaze to a woman, dressed in black, who was approaching from my right. It was obvious that the woman, whoever she was, had not been in the church.

"I don't want you here!" Lesley took a step towards her.

Everyone stared at the woman, and I overheard a number of whispered comments that made it clear this was Lucy Hannah, Dale Thomas's secretary. The woman hesitated for a moment, but then turned and walked away without a word.

The rest of the ceremony went without incident.

I waited until everyone had left, and then reversed the 'invisible' spell. I hated funerals, but it had been worthwhile attending just to see Lesley Thomas's reaction to Lucy Hannah. Perhaps the Thomas's marriage hadn't been as perfect as Lesley had painted it? I would have to speak to Lucy Hannah to try to get to the bottom of this.

***

The three witches were cackling inside the building. I was standing outside Magical Skincare, trying to decide how best to approach the situation. I could have used any number of spells to 'magic' myself inside, but why bother? Sometimes, the direct approach is best.

I pressed the buzzer on the front door, and the cackling stopped. I gave it a minute, and then pressed the buzzer again. This time I heard footsteps.

It was Giant Feet who answered the door. She wasn't wearing her witch garb. Instead, she was in heels and a grey suit, and looked every inch the receptionist.

"Can I help you?" She looked me up and down.

"Hiya." I engaged my ditzy, dumb blonde voice.

What do you mean? No, that isn't my normal voice. Cheek!

"Can I help you, young lady?"

"I'm here for the cream."

"Sorry?"

"The spot cream. I'm here for it."

"I'm sorry, but you've had a wasted journey. This is where Magical Skincare is manufactured, but we don't actually sell it from here. You'll need to buy it from a shop. There's a special offer on at The Central Mall today."

"Is that the one with the shark?"

"What shark?"

"Never mind. The cream they're selling there isn't strong enough. The spots keep coming back. I want some of the strong stuff."

"Sorry? I don't know what you mean."

"The stuff you keep in the cauldron. I thought I could dip my head in there."

"Who are you?"

"Your worst nightmare." I dropped the ditzy voice. "Out of my way." I pushed past her, and made my way into the room where The Wart and Tiny Witch were stirring the potion.

"Who are you?" The Wart turned on me.

"She just barged in," Giant Feet said.

"I'm Jill Gooder, and I'm here to tell you that if you don't shut down this operation by close of business today, I'll have a word with my good friend Daisy Flowers. You may know her as Daze."

"You're Mirabel's granddaughter, aren't you? You're that level seven witch?"

"That's me."

"Look, let's be reasonable. I've got a lot invested here. Maybe we could reach some kind of compromise? How about I cut you in for ten per cent?"

"Unbelievable."

"Okay, twenty then."

"I don't want your money. You're putting people's lives at risk with this stuff."

"Why do you care? They're only humans."

"Guess I'd better call Daze, then." I took out my phone.

"Wait! There's no need for that."

"Shut this lot down by close of business, or you'll get a visit from the rogue retrievers."

"Alright. I never did like the Milbright family. Too smart for their own good, all of them."

Chapter 12

I was all set to call in at the office when Aunt Lucy phoned, and asked me to go over there.

"Jill, can I introduce you to an old friend of mine. This is Archie."

The elf standing next to Aunt Lucy was dressed in a smart pin-stripe suit.

"Nice to meet you, Jill." He offered his hand. "Archie Bald."

"Archibald?"

"Actually, it's Archibald Bald, but all my friends call me Archie. Your aunt has told me a lot of good things about you. Or perhaps I should say 'gooder' things."

I managed a smile. If only I had a pound for every time I'd heard that.

"Archie is having a spot of bother, Jill." Aunt Lucy switched on the kettle. "I said you might be able to help. Why don't you two go through to the lounge while I make us all a nice cup of tea?"

"What seems to be the problem?" I asked, while Archie and I waited for Aunt Lucy to join us.

"I own a factory on Candlefield Industrial Estate: Elf Washing Machines. You may have heard of it?"

"I've come across washing machines with that name, but that was in Washbridge."

"They would be ours. We supply to both the sup and human worlds."

I didn't like to tell him that the only reason I'd heard of them was because both Kathy and Jen were having problems with leaks.

"My father started the business," Archie continued. "I took over a few years ago. Things were going from strength to strength until a couple of months back. Suddenly, we started to get lots of returns—a problem with leaks."

"I wasn't going to mention it, but my sister and a neighbour had exactly that problem with your machines."

"It's terrible." He shook his head. "Our reputation has taken a serious knock."

"I'm not sure how I can help. Isn't this a quality control issue?"

"If it was a QC problem, I would have solved it by now. I think this is sabotage."

"Do you have any proof?"

"None. That's why I need your help."

"Biscuit, Archie?" Aunt Lucy arrived with the tea.

"Do you have any custard creams?" he said.

"I only have two left at the moment, but I'm sure Jill won't mind if you have them, will you Jill?"

The last two? Couldn't he have had a ginger nut or something?

"Of course I don't mind." I almost choked on the words.

I missed some of what Archie said next because I was too distracted by watching him eating *my* custard creams.

"Do you think you'll be able to help me, Jill?" the custard cream thief said.

"Of course. I'll need to take a look at your factory."

"No problem. Here's my card. Just give me a call, and I'll make the necessary arrangements. I really do appreciate this."

***

Brent was in the outer office when I arrived.

"Jill. How are you feeling after yesterday?"

Mrs V looked concerned. "What happened yesterday?"

"Nothing, I just overdid it a little, didn't I, Brent?" I gave him a knowing look.

I didn't want him to tell her about my faux pas on the treadmill. She would think I was some kind of brainless klutz.

What do you mean it's a bit too late to worry about that?

"Err—yes, that's right." Brent looked a little confused, but thankfully, he played along. "Could I have a quick word, Jill?"

"Sure. Come through to my office."

"What's the cat doing?" Brent stared at Winky who was sitting on the window sill.

"He likes to look out of the window."

"What's that he's holding? It looks like a radio."

"That? It's just a toy that Jules bought for him. Now, what can I do for you?"

"Those men are back again next door. I thought I'd pop around to tell you, but I'll understand if you need some time to recover."

I was still nursing several bruises, but I wasn't about to let that stop me. "I'm fine. Give me two minutes, and I'll be there."

"Okay, thanks, Jill."

"Hey, you!" I yelled at Winky, once Brent had left.

"No need to shout. I'm not deaf."

"You can't use that radio when I have visitors."

"Roger that. Ten-four."

I got changed in record time, and made my way into the gym. The same four men were congregated at the far end of the room. This time, I planned to do what I should have done the previous day. I would use the 'listen' spell to eavesdrop on their conversation. If they were doing anything dodgy, I'd report back to Brent who could cancel their membership, and throw them out. Vampires could sometimes be a little tetchy, but they were unlikely to make a scene in broad daylight in a busy gym.

"Hi, Jill." The female voice distracted me.

"Maria?"

Luther's girlfriend looked amazing in her leotard, and judging by the sweat on her brow, she'd been working out pretty hard.

"Are you a member here?" she asked.

"Yeah. My office is just along the corridor."

"I joined yesterday." She leaned in, and spoke in a hushed voice. "I thought if I was going to be spending more time in the human world, that I'd better find somewhere to work out."

"Looks like you've had a hard session."

"It's the only way. We should work out together sometime."

"Yeah. That would be great." And would most likely be the death of me.

"I'll see you around then, Jill."

"Yeah. See you."

I expected her to head towards the changing room, but she walked over to the four men I'd been watching. I cast the 'listen' spell just in time to hear one of the male vampires say, "Ten pounds for a pint."

Maria reached inside the sports bag that she'd been carrying, and took out some cash, which she handed to him. In return, he gave her a bottle which Maria slipped into her bag. It didn't take a genius to work out what was in it.

The changing rooms were busy, so I didn't want to confront her in there. Instead I got changed and waited until Maria left. Then I followed her.

"Maria, wait!" I grabbed her arm as she was about to cross the road.

"Jill? What's wrong?"

"The bottle in your bag is what's wrong."

"You saw?"

"I've been watching those four. I knew they were up to something, but I didn't realise they were dealing in human blood. Have you started drinking it?"

"No, I promise. This is the first time I've ever bought any."

"But why?"

"I had no idea it would be so difficult to spend this much time in the human world. Being in such close contact with humans has awakened a longing in me that I didn't know existed. I was afraid I might do something stupid. I don't want to hurt anyone, and particularly not Luther."

"You've thought about biting Luther?"

"Yes. It's terrible. A couple of times I've found myself staring at his neck."

I was shocked, and didn't know what to say.

"Maybe it would be better if I just called it quits and went back to Candlefield?"

"There must be something else you can do. I know

Luther cares a lot about you."

"Does he, really?"

"Yes. He told me so, but he is concerned that you won't tell him where you live."

"How can I?"

"You can't—I understand that. But maybe, if you are serious about him, you should consider moving over here. If you're with humans all the time, you may get used to it more quickly."

"I suppose so."

"You need to make sure you have a good supply of synthetic blood at all times."

"You won't say anything to Luther, will you?"

"What would I tell him? That you're a vampire and I'm a witch?"

She managed a smile. "Thanks for being so understanding. I'm going to have to give this a lot of thought." She reached into her bag, and took out the bottle. "Here, you take this so I can't be tempted to drink it."

I took it from her, and then watched as she hurried away.

Poor Maria. This was going to be very difficult for her.

"Hi, Jill."

"Betty? I didn't see you there."

"What's in the bottle?"

"Which bottle?"

"The one in your hand."

"Oh, this bottle? It's—err—from The Final Straw. I got it 'to go'."

"What flavours did you choose?"

"Raspberry Revelation, Cherry Berry and Blackberry Blood."

"I've never heard of that last one."

"I think it's new."

"Can I have a taste?"

"Sorry." I moved it behind my back. "I have cold sores. I wouldn't want to pass them on to you."

"Oh? Okay. I'm glad I bumped into you, Jill. I have exciting news."

"Really?" I seriously doubted that.

"You'll never guess what. Norman is going to get his own premises. I'll have my shop back again, so it can go back to its original name. Isn't that fantastic?"

"Why is Norman moving out?"

"Two reasons, really. His sales are through the roof – much higher than he anticipated. He needs more room than is available in our little shop."

"Isn't it a bit risky to move to another shop so soon? Sales might not always stay at that level."

"You're right, and he probably wouldn't have made the move so quickly if it wasn't for reason number two."

"Which is?"

"His allergy has been playing up something rotten."

"Allergy to what?"

"Don't you remember? Norman is allergic to crustaceans. He thought the cream might help, but it hasn't. He spends all day scratching."

"Poor thing."

"So you see, he really didn't have any choice. He had to put some distance between himself and my crabs."

"Right. Well, tell him good luck from me."

"Will do."

"I'd better dash."

"Okay. I hope they get better soon, Jill."

"Sorry?"

"Your cold sores."

"Oh, yeah. Right. Bye."

***

Despite my best efforts to persuade him that we should give it a miss, Jack had dragged me to the talk at PAW. I'd even put on my sexiest nightie, and suggested we should have a night in, but he'd said we couldn't let Mrs Rollo and Marco down.

Men? I'd never understand them.

PAW held their meetings in an old church hall on the west side of Washbridge Park. Mrs Rollo had gone on ahead with Marco. By the time Jack and I arrived there, it was standing room only.

"It's too crowded," I said. "We'll never see anything. Let's go home."

"It's okay, look." Jack pointed. "Mrs Rollo has saved us some seats. We're on the front row."

"Great." I had hoped that I might be able to nod off without anyone noticing, but there was no chance of that now we were at the front.

The atmosphere in the room was electric. Everyone seemed excited for the upcoming talk. Everyone except me.

"Have you seen any?" The old man sitting next to me tapped my arm.

"Sorry? Any what?"

"Ghosts? Or vampires?"

"No, I don't really believe in —"

"I saw a werewolf once."

"Really?" I turned to Jack, and whispered, "Swap places."

"I can't. I'm talking to Mrs Rollo."

"He was emptying the bins," the crazy old man continued.

"Who was?"

"The werewolf."

"How could you tell he was a werewolf?"

"By the way he picked up the bins. Two at a time."

"Maybe he just worked out?"

"No. He was definitely a werewolf. You can't fool old Joey. That's me. Nice to meet you." He offered me his hand.

"Jill Gooder." I smiled, but passed on the hand shake. His fingernails could have cultivated a nice crop of potatoes.

"Ladies and gentlemen." A young man was now standing at the front of the room. "Welcome to Paranormal Activity Watch. I'm Greg Lewis. It's quite a turnout we have today. I'm not sure I've ever seen so many people here. Tonight, we're honoured to have with us one of the leading paranormal activity experts from Australia. Fresh from his travels, I give you Marco Rollo."

I laughed. Fortunately, only Jack heard me because everyone else was too busy clapping.

"What's wrong with you, Jill?" He gave me one of his disapproving looks.

"Marco Rollo? Fresh from his travels?" I laughed again. "Come on, that's funny!"

"I don't get it?" Jack shook his head.

Sheesh! What was wrong with people?

"Thank you, Greg." Marco took centre stage. "I'm honoured to have been asked here today."

And with that, he launched into a two hour bore-athon on all things paranormal. It wouldn't have been so bad if he hadn't insisted on churning out so many statistics. Did we know that Washbridge had precisely six point-three times the mean number of paranormal activity reports? Surely, the more pertinent question would have been, did anyone care? Needless to say, my response would have been a resounding 'No'. But, I would have been in a minority of one. Everyone else in that room hung on every word that spewed out of Marco's mouth. Me? I was playing paranormal-cliché bingo. Not that anyone cared.

I laughed again. Much louder this time. Everyone stared at me.

"What's wrong with you?" Jack said under his breath. He was clearly embarrassed to be seated next to such a childish idiot.

"Look at that graph!" I pointed.

Marco had helpfully illustrated his talk with a series of graphs. This particular line chart reminded me of something.

"It looks like a witch's hat. Look, there's the point."

"Grow up, Jill," Jack scolded.

That had told me. I sat in silence for the next two millennia. When Marco finally brought the torture to an end, I clapped louder than anyone. The relief was so great.

I was just about to stand up when Greg took the floor again.

"Thank you, Marco. That was fascinating. And now, before we call it a day, there's just one other item on the agenda."

Great!

"Today, I took delivery of the CZ 651." He lifted a small machine onto the table in front of him. "This is the last word in paranormal activity meters."

There was a collective 'oooh' in the room, but not from me. I wasn't sure I liked the sound of this. Not one bit.

"With this little beauty," he continued, "I'll be able to pick up even the lowest levels of paranormal activity."

"Give us a demonstration," someone shouted.

No, don't.

"Yeah, give us a demonstration, Greg," Marco said. "Maybe there's a ghost in this room right now."

"Okay." Greg was obviously dying to play with his new toy. "Just a quick one, though."

I began to cough, and grabbed my throat.

"Are you okay?" Jack looked concerned.

I coughed louder. It was another Oscar worthy performance from Jill Gooder.

"Jill? Are you alright?"

I got up from my seat, and hurried to the exit door. Jack followed.

Once outside, I kept up the act for a couple of minutes, and then took a deep breath. "I'm okay."

"Are you sure?" Jack put his arm around me. "What happened?"

"No idea. I'm alright now. Sorry about that."

Just then, the crowd started to pile out of the building.

"Are you okay, Jill?" Mrs Rollo was standing next to me.

"Fine thanks. I was just choking. Did we miss anything?"

"Yes, actually. Greg said he'd detected some activity, but it was very weak."

"How strange."

Chapter 13

Jack was eating muesli.

Yuk! Does anyone actually like that horrible stuff?

What? You do? Freak!

I was on my second slice of toast. The night before, I'd hidden the bread in the crockery cupboard, just in case Jack decided to steal it for a suppertime sandwich.

"Why didn't you tell me you were a witch?" he said.

I almost choked. How had he found out? What should I do now?

"Why else would you have sneaked out of PAW last night?" He laughed. "Or maybe, you're a vampire."

"You got me. I'm a vampire. Oh, and thanks for the sympathy. I did almost choke to death last night."

"Sorry. I thought that gizmo that he had was incredible."

"You don't seriously believe that thing actually works, do you?"

"Why not? In fact, I found the whole evening fascinating. I might start to go to the PAW meetings."

"Please tell me you're joking. Surely one sad hobby is enough for anyone?"

"There's nothing sad about ten-pin bowling."

"There is the way you play it."

"What's wrong with having interests and hobbies? All you ever do is work. You know what they say about all work and no play, don't you?"

"That it makes you a dull boy?"

Jack was ready to leave before I was.

"I might be late in tonight." He gave me a peck on the

lips.

"Ghost hunting?"

"Nothing so exciting. I have training for most of the day, so I'll need to catch up on a few things afterwards. I'll get my own dinner."

"Okay. See you later."

Although I'd made light of it, I wasn't at all thrilled at the prospect of Jack joining PAW. It was already difficult enough living with a human.

When I left the house, Megan was just coming out of her door.

"Morning, Jill."

"Morning." I walked over to her. "I just wanted to say that was a really nice thing you did—withdrawing from the Washbridge House contract."

"To tell you the truth, I'm glad I did. I'm not ready to take on something as big as that yet. Maybe in a couple of years."

"You did it for Peter, though, didn't you?"

"I was in two minds anyway, but when I realised it was Peter who I was up against, that made my decision for me."

"He and Kathy are very grateful."

"Does that mean she doesn't hate me anymore?"

"Of course not. Are you over Harry?"

"Who?" She laughed. "If I tell you something, do you promise not to repeat it to anyone?"

"Of course. Discretion is my middle name."

What? You were expecting that same joke again, weren't you? Come on, I'm better than that.

"I've signed up with a dating agency." Megan blushed a little.

"Really? I can't believe you need to do that. You must have guys throwing themselves at you."

"Yeah, but they're all losers, like Harry. I want to find someone with the right personality, and I thought I might have a better chance this way. And besides, my accountant recommended this dating agency. He's just found himself a lovely girlfriend through it."

It couldn't be, could it?

"Your accountant, what's his name?"

"Luther Stone."

"Small world. Luther's my accountant too."

"No way. He's hot, isn't he?"

"I can't say I've ever noticed," I lied.

"I had a thing for him when he first started doing my books back when I was just modelling, but he never showed any interest. He was dating someone who was into sea shells or something."

"So, I take it you've signed up with Love Bites?"

"That's right. I'm still waiting for my first match. It's really exciting." She glanced up the street. "Oh, no!"

I followed her gaze, and saw Mr Hosey's train heading down the road.

"See you, Jill." Megan jumped into her van, and reversed off the drive at breakneck speed.

Unfortunately, I wasn't quick enough. Bessie was now parked across my driveway.

"Morning, Jill." Mr Hosey tooted his whistle.

"Morning. I'm just on my way to work." I gestured to the train. "If you could maybe move it out of the way?"

"Morning, Jill." Mr Ivers stuck his head out of one of the carriages.

"Morning, Mr Ivers. Taking advantage of your free

rides, I see."

"Of course. I can't get enough of Bessie."

"Like I said to Mr Hosey, I have to get to work."

"You missed a golden opportunity with the sponsorship of this little beauty."

"Really? Have you landed some new subscribers?"

"Not yet, but it's looking promising. A number of people have come out of their houses to ask what it's all about."

"Right. Were you by any chance parked in front of their driveways at the time?"

"Yes. How did you know?"

"Just a wild guess. And did they shout something like, 'what's this all about'?"

"That's right. I'm going to get some flyers printed so I can hand them out in future."

"Great plan."

***

Imelda Barrowtop's Will was to be read in the offices of Day, Day, Day, Day & Week, solicitors. The receptionist, a blur of brunette curls, had earphones in. I couldn't be sure if she was transcribing notes, or listening to Spotify. I had to wave my hand in front of her nose to get her attention.

"Jill Gooder. I'm here for the reading of Imelda Barrowtop's Will."

"Take a seat over there, please."

"Where are the others?"

"You're the only one so far."

"Who will be dealing with this matter, today?"

"Mr Twoday."

"Today, yes. Who is dealing with it?"

"Mr Twoday."

Why was nothing ever easy?

"I want to know his name."

"I just told you. Mr Twoday. That's T-W-O-D-A-Y."

"Oh, I see. So, you have a Twoday, four Days and a Week, then?"

"Actually, there are now five Days. Justin Day has just joined the firm. We're waiting for the sign to be changed."

"Why don't you just shorten the name on the sign to 'Fortnight'?"

"Sorry?"

"You have a Twoday, five Days and a Week. That's a fortnight." I laughed.

"Oh yes. Very good," she said, stony-faced. "If you could just take a seat over there?"

"Morning, Jill." Imelda Barrowtop's daughter, Petunia, took a seat next to me.

"Morning. I'm the only one here so far."

"It's only going to be you and me."

"Oh? I thought—"

Just then, the door to our left opened, and a wizard with a shiny forehead appeared.

"Morning, ladies. I'm Sunny Twoday. Would you care to follow me?"

He led the way to a small office with his name on the door.

Did you notice how I didn't mock his name? It took a lot of self-restraint, I'll have you know.

"This shouldn't take very long," Mr Twoday said, once we were all seated. "This is the last Will and Testament of

Mrs Imelda Barrowtop: I, Imelda Barrowtop, being of sound mind, do leave all of my other-worldly possessions to my daughter Petunia, with the exception of the journal which I have placed in safekeeping at the offices of Day & Week." Mr Twoday hesitated. "This Will was written quite some time ago when there was only the one Mr Day." With that explanation to one side, he continued, "I bequeath this journal to Magna Mondale, or in the event that Magna should predecease me, then it should pass to whoever is in possession of Magna Mondale's book." He turned to me. "I understand from Petunia that you have that book?"

"Actually, no."

"I thought you did?" Petunia said.

"I retrieved it from the sealed room, but it's no longer in my possession."

"That's very unfortunate," Mr Twoday said. "I can't give you the journal unless I have sight of Magna Mondale's book."

"Do you know what's in your mother's journal?" I asked Petunia, once we were back outside.

"No idea. I didn't even know it existed. I'm sorry I wasted your time, today, Jill."

"Don't give it a second thought. Would you like to get a coffee or something?"

"Thanks, but I'd prefer to get back home."

"Okay. Bye, Petunia."

***

I'd arranged to meet with Dale Thomas's secretary,

Lucy Hannah, at her apartment, which was only a stone's throw from Central Mall. She answered the door, dressed in jeans and a baggy jumper.

"Ms Hannah?"

"Please call me Lucy. Come in."

She led the way into a lounge which looked out over the main entrance to the mall.

"You must have noticed an increase in traffic since that opened?"

"I have. I may have to look for somewhere new. It took me an additional fifteen minutes to get home yesterday."

"It can't be fun staring out at that shark all day long."

"What shark?"

"The giant one above the sign."

She glanced out of the window. "Oh, yeah. I hadn't noticed that."

Sheesh.

"What happened at the funeral must have been very difficult for you?" I said.

"You were there?"

"I was close by."

"I didn't want to cause a scene; that's why I didn't attend the church service. But I thought I might at least get to say goodbye to Dale when they lowered—" She grabbed a tissue and patted her eyes. "Sorry."

"Were you and Dale—err—close?"

"By 'close', I assume you mean were we having an affair? No, we weren't. Dale and I were friends—good friends—but never more than that."

"It looked as though Lesley thought there was more to it."

"She knew he and I were close, and assumed the worst.

Dale was there for me during a particularly difficult time in my life. I'm not sure I would have got through it without him. He deserved much better than her. She was the one having an affair. Did you know that?"

"I didn't. Do you know who with?"

"No. Dale was sure she was seeing someone, but he didn't know who it was. In fact, only recently, he told me he was thinking of getting a P.I. to follow her."

"Did he actually hire someone?"

"I don't think so."

"Do you think it's possible that he might have been depressed because of this business with his wife?"

"He wasn't happy about it, but he wasn't suicidal, if that's what you mean. I've heard reports that it might have been suicide. That's impossible. One hundred per cent impossible. Dale loved life, even if he was unhappy with his marriage."

"The medical examiner said he had no pre-existing medical conditions. Had he seemed okay to you in the days before it happened?"

"Yes, he was as fit as a fiddle. That's why I find the idea of him blacking out hard to believe. Why are you investigating his death, anyway? Do you think there might have been foul play?"

"I have an open mind, but so far, I have found nothing to suggest that it was anything but an accident."

"You should take a closer look at Lesley. She was in the aeroplane too, wasn't she? She must have done something to him."

My meeting with Lucy Hannah had been worthwhile because I'd learned that Dale Thomas had suspected his wife of having an affair. Had he been right? Sometimes jealousy can cause people to see things that aren't there. If she was cheating, who was she seeing? Maybe Dale's business partner would be able to shed some light on that. He was next on my list of people to talk to. I'd already tried to contact him a couple of times, but without any luck. It was time to be a little more persistent.

Chapter 14

I grabbed lunch at Chicken Bits. Not the greatest name for a shop, but their crispy chicken nuggets were to die for.

"You've got sauce around your mouth." Mrs V admonished me when I arrived at the office.

"I've just had nuggets." I took a tissue from my bag and wiped my mouth.

"You've missed a bit." She touched her upper lip. "That's it. I really don't know why you buy that stuff, Jill. It isn't good for you."

"Chicken is healthy."

"The stuff they cook it in isn't. You should eat a few salads."

Yeah. Right. Like that was ever going to happen.

"Anything to report, Mrs V? Have I had dozens of calls from prospective clients?"

"Not exactly dozens."

"Some though?"

"There was one call."

"What was that?"

"Someone wanting to know whether we stocked Ethernet cable."

I sighed.

"I do have some news, though," she said. "You know I mentioned that I was going to look for voluntary work? Well, I've found something. It's only one day per week, but it's a start."

"That's great. What is it?"

"Wheels on meals."

I laughed. "You mean meals on wheels."

"I know what I mean, Jill. Wheels on meals is nothing like meals on wheels. They're based at Washbridge Social Centre. It provides meals for the senior citizens who are mobile enough to make it into the city. The meals are heavily subsidised, so it's very popular as you might imagine. So popular, in fact, that the queuing times had become ridiculously long. All that standing around can be very difficult for some of the old people—their legs aren't what they used to be. That's when they came up with the ingenious idea of wheels on meals. Under this new system, there's no need to queue. The diners simply take a seat at a table, and when the meals are ready, they're placed onto a plate on a tray, which has wheels on it. The trays are then pushed across the floor to the diner."

"This is a wind-up, isn't it? You almost had me going there with your 'wheels on meals'."

"It isn't a joke, Jill. It's a brilliant scheme."

"Aren't there lots of spillages as the meals shoot across the floor?"

"Very few, actually, but that's because the wheelies undergo weeks of training."

"Hold on. The wheelies?"

"That's what they call the staff who have been trained to propel the meals across the floor."

"So, are you a wheelie?"

"Of course not. I've only just started there. I just put the meals on the trays at the moment, but I am hoping to eventually become a wheelie."

"Well, I have to say Mrs V. That all sounds *wheelie* great. I'm *wheelie* impressed."

She sighed, clearly not amused.

***

Leo Riley burst into my office with Mrs V once again in hot pursuit. This was becoming a habit, and not one I was very happy about.

"We need to talk!" he yelled.

"Just a second. Let me check my diary. How does next Friday sound?"

"We need to talk right now!"

"Thanks Mrs V. I'll take it from here."

She gave Riley one of the looks that she usually reserved for Winky.

"Care for a seat, Leo?"

"It's Detective Riley, and no, I prefer to stand."

"As you wish. Is something troubling you?"

"Someone has been impersonating me."

"Well, you know what they say: Imitation is the sincerest —"

"This isn't a laughing matter."

"Apparently not. Why come to see me about it?"

"Someone went to see the accident investigator and the medical examiner who are working on the Thomas case."

"Isn't that the skydiving death?"

"You know very well it is. I know that you've been hired to investigate this by a friend of the deceased."

"How do you know that?" Was someone leaking information from my office? Winky perhaps? A couple of tins of salmon would be enough to bribe him.

"Never mind how I know. The accident investigator and the medical examiner are off limits."

"Attractive, isn't she?"

"Who?"

"The medical examiner. I've seen her photograph in The Bugle. Now, what was her name? Top, Tops, something like that."

"Sheila Treetop."

"That's it. Look, Leo—sorry—Detective Riley—I'm confused. How am I supposed to have passed myself off as you? In case you hadn't noticed, I'm a woman."

"You must have got an accomplice to do it for you."

"You got me." I held up my hands. "I persuaded my cat to impersonate you."

Riley was red in the face and breathing so heavily that I thought he might have a coronary.

"I know you're behind this Gooder, and as soon as I can prove it, you'll be behind bars." With that, he stomped out of the room.

After Riley had left, Winky jumped onto my desk.

"I thought that guy's head was going to explode," he said.

"Excitable chap, isn't he?"

"You shouldn't have to put up with that kind of thing. Would you like a neck massage? It might relieve the tension."

"No, I'm good, thanks."

"Okay, but if there's anything you need, just give me a shout."

That cat was definitely up to something.

***

Before I started my investigation into the issues being encountered by Elf Washing Machines, I needed to get a feel for the scale of the problem. Kathy and Jen had both been sold lemons, but were they just unlucky, or was the problem endemic?

I'd contacted Kathy who'd told me she bought her machine from Whyte Goods. I'd expected it to be one of those sprawling superstores, but instead Whyte Goods turned out to be a small shop a few doors down from The Howling pub.

"Good afternoon, madam." A man in a smart suit greeted me.

"Hi."

"I'm Westly Whyte, the owner. Was there anything in particular that you're looking for today?"

"Actually, I'm just after some information."

"If I can help, I will."

"My sister and one of my neighbours recently had a problem with their Elf washing machines."

"A leak from the door?"

"You've had other customers with the same problem?"

"Too many, I'm afraid. The strange thing is we've carried Elf washing machines for years, and never had a single problem before, but over these last few months there have been at least eight, to my knowledge. I'm loathe to do it, but if it continues, I'll have to give serious consideration to dropping that brand."

"Have you heard of any other shops encountering similar problems with them?"

"I know of at least two, but if you're in the market for a washing machine, there are a couple of other brands I can highly recommend."

"No, that's okay, thanks. You've been most helpful."

None of this boded well for Archie Bald. Whatever the problem was, it was obviously widespread. If retailers in the human world lost faith in the brand, it might spell the end for Elf Washing Machines.

It was time I took a look inside the factory.

***

Jack was doing some training at work, and expected to be late in. That was excuse enough for me to order in takeout. There was no point in cooking a meal for one.

Who are you calling lazy?

As always, I called 'One Minute Takeaway', and as always, they were at my door within sixty seconds. That's what I call service.

The pizza was delicious and hit the mark nicely. Now, what should I have for dessert? There was just one piece of gateau left in the fridge. Jack and I had eaten the rest at the weekend. I'd had two pieces to his one, which by my reckoning meant this last piece must be mine.

Snigger.

Before I could get it out of the fridge, there was a knock at the door.

"Jill!" The young woman beamed. She obviously knew me, but I didn't have a clue who she was.

"Hi?"

"Long time no see."

"Err—yeah?"

"Come to think of it, we didn't actually meet each other back then. We just had the photographs, didn't we?"

"Did we?" Who was this woman?

"It was all handwritten letters. Not much email or

texting when we were kids, was there?"

"Look, I'm terribly sorry, but I can't quite place you."

"It's Rosy Glass. Your penfriend!"

Oh bum!

"Rosy? What a surprise."

"Isn't it? You could have knocked me down with a feather when your sister got in touch."

"Kathy contacted you?"

"Yeah. She phoned me a couple of days ago, and said that you and she had been reminiscing about the good old days, and that you'd been talking about me. Kathy said you wished we'd kept in touch. That's why she sought me out, and sent me an email. Wasn't that a nice thing to do?"

"Really nice." Kathy was sooo dead. "Fancy you living nearby."

"Oh, I don't. I live on the Isle of Skye."

"Isn't that a long way away?"

"Two trains, a bus and two taxis. I thought I'd never get here."

It was only then that I spotted the suitcase at her feet.

"Where are you staying, Rosy?"

"I—err—I—suppose I could try to find a hotel." She gave me a puppy dog look. "I might still have enough money left."

"You must stay with us."

Had I really just said that?

"That's incredibly generous." She practically barged me out of the way on her way in. "This is a lovely place you have here. Kathy said you lived with a policeman?"

"Jack. That's right. He has to work late tonight."

"That's lucky. It'll give us time to catch up."

Yay! "I guess so."

"What shall I do with my case?"

"The spare bedroom is kind of full, and there's no bed in there."

"No problem. I can sleep on the sofa. You won't know I'm here." She took out a handkerchief, and blew her nose so loudly that Jack's bowling trophy rocked on the mantelpiece.

"Would you mind if I took a shower, Jill?"

"Sure. Upstairs, second on the left."

"When I come down, we can talk about old times."

"Great!"

I waited until I heard the shower running, and then got on the phone.

"I'm going to kill you, Kathy!"

"Is that my loving sister?"

"How could you?"

"You're going to have to give me more than that."

"Rosy Glass!"

She laughed. "Oh dear. Did she call you?"

"No, she didn't call me. She's in my shower."

Kathy could barely speak for laughing. "Are you joking?"

"Do I sound like I'm joking?"

"I'm sorry. I got a little carried away. After we'd been talking about her, I thought it would be funny to look her up. I had no idea she'd pay you a visit."

"Well she did."

"She probably won't stay long."

"Oh, is that right? She lives on the Isle of Skye. It took her all day to get here, and she has a suitcase with her."

All I could hear was laughter.

"Kathy!"

"Sorry. Look, Pete's just come in. I have to go."

"Kathy wait!"

She'd hung up.

"I'm home!" Jack was back much earlier than I'd expected. "How was your day?" He gave me a kiss.

"Okay until a few minutes ago."

"Why?"

Just then, Rosy walked across the landing, and started down the stairs.

"Who's that?"

"That's Rosy."

"Who?"

"You must be Jack." Rosy appeared in the doorway. "Pleased to meet you."

Jack offered his hand; Rosy ignored it, and went in for the hug.

"Who is she?" he mouthed over her shoulder.

"Jack. This is Rosy Glass."

Rosy pulled back. "We used to be penfriends, didn't we Jill?"

"We certainly did. Kathy contacted Rosy, and told her where I live."

"Did she?" Jack gave me a look. "That was nice of her."

"Wasn't it?" Rosy gushed. "Jill said I could sleep on the sofa."

"Oh?" He looked at me for an explanation.

"Rosy has travelled all the way from the Isle of Skye."

"That is a long way," he said.

"Is it okay if I make a cup of tea?" Rosy was wiping her wet hair.

"Sure. Help yourself."

As soon as she'd left the room, Jack turned to me.

"What's going on?"

"This is all Kathy's fault. When we had our night in, we got talking about my old penfriend. The stupid idiot only went and tracked Rosy down, and emailed her."

"What possessed her to travel all this way?"

"I don't know, but I could hardly kick her out, could I?"

"How long will she be staying?"

"Not long. I hope."

"I hope you don't mind, Jill." Rosy appeared at the door with a cup of tea in her hand. "I've just eaten the last two custard creams."

"No, of course not," I said, through clenched teeth.

"Oh, I've just remembered." Rosy put down the tea, and opened her suitcase. "I bought you a present."

"You really shouldn't have."

"I wanted to. I know how interested you used to be in these."

"A ship in a bottle? How very nice."

Chapter 15

"Shush! She'll hear you," I said, in a hushed voice.

It was the next morning. Jack and I had showered and dressed, but were still in the bedroom.

"How long do you think she'll stay?" he said, in a whisper.

"I've no idea, but she's brought a suitcase with her, so she must be expecting to be here for a while."

"How come you've never talked about her before?"

"I'd forgotten all about her until Kathy mentioned her the other night. That sister of mine is so dead."

"I'm starving." Jack started for the door. "Are you coming down?"

I followed him down the stairs, half expecting to find Rosy fast asleep on the sofa. I would have to have a talk with her to try to find out how long she was planning to stay.

"Jack, Jill, I was going to leave you a note." Rosy was dressed, and had her suitcase in her hand. Had she overheard us talking about her? "I'm really sorry, but I have to leave straight away."

Yay and double yay! "How disappointing. You've only just arrived."

"I know, and I feel terrible about this. You've both made me so welcome, but I've had a phone call—there's an emergency at work."

"Where do you work?" Jack asked.

"At the stick insect sanctuary."

I laughed, but then realised she wasn't joking. "Sorry, I was thinking about something Jack said just now. What's wrong at the stick—err—at your work?"

"I left Lydia, my second in command, in charge while I came down here. Apparently, she put her back out while taking out the trash. There's no one to look after the stickies."

"Stickies?"

"That's what I call the stick insects."

"Of course." I was barely holding it together. "It's a pity you have to leave so soon."

"Do you have the number of a local taxi firm?"

"No need to call a taxi. Jack will run you to the station, won't you?"

"Of course. I'll just get some breakfast first."

"My train leaves in twenty minutes," Rosy said.

"In that case, you'd better go now, Jack." I gave him a loving smile.

He gave me a snarl in return.

"I hope I'll be able to get down here again sometime," Rosy managed, through her tears.

"Me too. Next time, though, give me a call first."

"Or you could come up to Skye? I'd love to show you around the sanctuary."

"Sounds great. You'd better hurry or you'll miss your train."

Rosy headed out of the door.

"See you tonight, sugar pie." I blew Jack a kiss on his way out. "I'm just going to get my breakfast."

***

I'd had a phone call from F For Print, to say that my order was ready.

"Are these okay?" Fred held one up.

"Oh yes. They're just perfect. Thanks."

As soon as I was out of the shop, I magicked myself over to Candlefield. It was early, and there was hardly anyone about, which was ideal for my purposes. There was no time to lose. I had a lot of ground to cover.

"Jill?" Amber looked surprised to see me when I rolled into Cuppy C an hour later. "You look bushed. Are you okay?"

"Never better. A cup of tea and two slices of toast, please."

"What? No muffin?"

"I do eat other things."

"Really? I've never seen you."

"Are you excited about London, Jill?" Pearl had come through from the cake shop.

"I haven't really had the chance to think much about it. I've been really busy."

"Us too, haven't we, Amber?"

"Run off our feet."

I suspected that my idea of 'being busy', and the twins' idea of 'being busy', were miles apart.

"It's my interview on Candle TV this morning." I grimaced.

"Rather you than me." Amber put two slices of bread in the toaster.

"Yeah. She's horrible, that Eileen whatshername."

"Eclair? She doesn't scare me."

"What are they going to ask you?" Pearl said.

"They sent me a list of questions." I took the sheet of paper out of my bag, and handed it to Pearl.

"Have you planned your answers?"

"No. I started to, but figured it would be obvious that I had, so I plan on winging it."

Amber took the list of questions from her sister. "This looks like some kind of witch hunt."

"It'll be fine. It's not like I have anything to hide, is it?" In truth, I wasn't feeling anywhere near as confident or relaxed as I was trying to appear. Given a choice, I would have declined to take part in the interview, but I knew that would solve nothing. They would just continue to pursue me relentlessly.

"How dare you?" Miles Best came charging into the shop. He was red in the face, and unless I was very much mistaken, he was not happy about something.

Snigger!

"Morning, Miles." I flashed him a smile. "Cup of tea?"

"I don't want a drink. What do you think you're playing at, Jill?"

"I have no idea what you're talking about."

"You know very well." He half unrolled the poster he had in his hand. "I'm talking about this."

Amber and Pearl both giggled.

"I can't see it all." I snatched it from his hand, and unrolled it fully. "Oh dear." I laughed.

It was impossible to tell if Miles' red face was caused by anger or embarrassment—probably both.

"Give me that!" He tried to snatch it back, but I was too quick for him.

The poster showed the cartoon-like body of an overweight naked man, standing with his back to the viewer. The man, who had Miles Best's face, was looking over his shoulder. All in all, it was not a pretty sight.

"Looks like you need to cut back on the muffins." Pearl managed through tears of laughter.

"You should probably think about working out more." Amber too was in hysterics.

"You've stuck my head on this body!" Miles pointed an accusing finger at me.

"Me?" Cue little Miss Innocent. "I don't know anything about it."

"That is not my body!" He insisted.

"There's one easy way to prove it. Show us your bum, Miles."

He was practically foaming at the mouth. "I'll get you for this! All of you!"

And with that, he stormed out of the shop.

"Too funny!" Amber said.

"Where did you put the poster?" Pearl was still struggling to get her breath.

"On the wall outside Best Cakes." I grinned. "And on every other flat surface I could find around Candlefield market place."

***

Despite my show of bravado in front of the twins, I was really nervous about the TV interview.

"This way, Jill." The chatty, smiling production assistant had told me her name, but it hadn't registered. "You've just got time for makeup."

"Makeup? Don't I look okay?" I'd spent twice as much time as usual putting on my makeup that morning, in preparation for the interview.

"You look fine, but we just need to make sure you don't

'glow' on camera. It will only take a minute." She led the way into a small dressing room where a young male wizard was waiting, makeup brush in hand.

He took one look at me, and then turned to the production assistant. "What am I supposed to do with *this*, Ginny? I've told you before I need at least twenty minutes."

"I'm sorry, Seb, but she only just got here. You've got five minutes."

"I'll do what I can." He sighed deeply. "But I can't work miracles."

By now, what little confidence I'd had, had ebbed away.

Seb did his thing, and then Ginny grabbed my arm, and led me through to the studio where I was told to sit on the red leather couch. Behind the three cameras, which were pointed straight at me, was a gaggle of technicians and cameramen, all talking in hushed voices. I was relieved to see there wasn't going to be a live studio audience.

"Attention studio!" A voice came through the speakers. "We go live in ten. To your positions, please. Opening credits roll. Good luck, everyone."

From nowhere, Eclair appeared, and took a seat next to me on the sofa.

"Good morning, everyone," she said into the camera. "Welcome to this very special edition of Candle Investigates. My guest this morning is someone who will already be known to many in the sup community, particularly to the witches. Jill Gooder was raised in the human world, and was apparently oblivious to the fact that she was a witch. Since joining the sup community, her rise to fame has been nothing short of amazing. Today, I hope to get answers to some of the questions that we all have." Eclair turned around to face me. "Jill, welcome. Thank you for joining us this morning."

Like I had a choice. "My pleasure."

"If I may, I'd like to start with an incident that has recently come to light. I understand that you were invited to give a talk at Candlefield Academy of Supernatural Studies?"

"That's right, Ecla—err—Eileen. I was asked to talk about what it's like to live in the human world."

"A great honour, I'm sure. I understand that while you were there, something happened to one of the young pupils. Maybe you could tell the viewers about that?"

"A pouchfeeder breached the walls and grabbed a young boy named Tommy. Fortunately, we were able to stop the creature taking the boy back to its nest."

"I believe you played a major part in thwarting the creature's escape?"

"I helped."

"Jill, you're being far too modest. From what I've heard, the creature would have got away with the boy if you hadn't intercepted it by using a secret passageway. Isn't that true?"

I nodded.

"The question is, Jill: How did you know about that passageway when no one else at the school was aware of its existence?"

"I don't know. I just did."

She turned to the camera. "*You just did?*" Then back to me. "That's not really an answer, is it, Jill?"

"I don't know what else I can tell you. That's the truth."

"I see. Maybe we should move onto another issue of interest to our viewers. How did you get inside Magna

Mondale's sealed room? That room had been sealed for ages, and many witches had tried to gain access before you. And yet you, a mere level two witch at the time, managed to get inside."

"I simply focussed all my energy on making the door open."

"And it did? Just like that? And yet numerous level six witches before you had tried, but failed. Don't you find that rather strange?"

"Very. I don't know why I succeeded."

"Really?" She looked again into the camera, sighed, and then turned back to me. "Perhaps the most interesting part of your journey so far is the twenty plus years that you lived in the human world. Are we really supposed to believe that during all of that time you didn't realise you were a witch?"

"It's true. My birth mother told me on her deathbed. Until then, I had no idea."

"I see. So, you're saying that when this dying woman, who you'd never seen since the day you were born, told you that you were a witch, you simply accepted it?"

"No. I didn't. At the time, I thought she'd said it as an insult."

"You thought that being called a witch was an insult?"

"You have to remember I thought I was a human. Humans sometimes call a woman a witch if they want to insult her."

"We'll have to take your word for that. But, even though you initially thought it was an insult, you eventually accepted that you were indeed a sup?"

"Yes, because I realised that I was able to perform spells. I could hardly deny who I was after that, could I?"

"Okay. We're nearly out of time. Can you explain how someone, who for over twenty years didn't even know she was a witch, has managed to progress up the levels quicker than any other witch in living memory?"

"I don't know. I did put a lot of effort into learning the spells."

"*A lot of effort*? Of course, that would explain it. I'm sure no one else has thought of doing that."

"No, that's not what I meant."

"Let me sum up what you've told us this morning. *You don't know* how you knew about the secret passageway at CASS, *you don't know* how you got into Magna Mondale's sealed room, and *you don't know* how you progressed through the levels quicker than any other witch. *You don't know* much of anything, do you, Jill?"

Before I could respond, she turned to the camera. "So, viewers, there you have it. What are we to make of Jill Gooder? That's for you to decide. Thank you for watching this morning. I'll see you the same time tomorrow."

The voice came through the speakers again, "That's it, everyone. Great job, Eileen."

Eclair turned to me, all smiles. "Thanks, Jill. I thought that went really well."

And with that, she disappeared backstage.

Chapter 16

My head was still spinning when I got out of the TV studio. I'd been naive to think I could handle Eclair so easily. She was a pro, and had ambushed me in the most spectacular style.

And yet, it wasn't Eclair or the interview that was causing my head to spin. It was the reality of what she had said. The interview had crystallised my own thoughts, and they could be summed up in three words. The same three words that Eclair had used at the end of the interview: *I didn't know.*

There was so much about my own life that I didn't know or understand. I had often worried that Jack was in the dark about a large part of my life, but the truth was, so was I. How had I known about the passageway at CASS? How had I been able to get into Magna Mondale's sealed room? How had I progressed so quickly up the levels? How had I lived as a human for so many years without realising I was a witch?

I didn't know, but it was well past time that I found some answers.

***

I magicked myself back to Washbridge. Jules was behind the desk.

"Hi, Jill."

"Any messages?"

"Just one. A man wanted to know if we sell Routers."

"Right."

"Are you okay, Jill? You seem a little down."

"I'm alright. I've just had a busy morning."

"I have some good news."

"I could use some."

"Gilbert's back to his old self. He came over to see me last night, and he was bright and chatty, just like he used to be."

"That's really great."

"It's not all good, though."

"Oh?"

"Magical Skincare has closed down, so he's out of a job."

"I'm sure he'll find another one soon."

"That's what I told him. That's not all, though. His acne has come back, and it's worse than ever."

"Oh dear."

"I don't mind. I'd rather he had a few spots than act like a zombie."

***

"Hi, Jill." Winky greeted me as soon as I walked into my office. "You're looking particularly radiant today."

My suspicionometer jumped into the red again. What was with the compliments? Normally, whenever I stepped through the door, he either ignored me, or pestered me to feed him.

There was a brochure open on my desk. Had Jules left it there?

Purrfect Cruises? That didn't sound like something Jules would have been looking at, but I had a sneaking suspicion I knew who it did belong to.

"Is this yours, Winky?"

"Oh?" He feigned surprise. "I didn't realise I'd left it there."

A likely story.

"What do you think?" He jumped onto the desk. "About that cruise."

"The one on the page you just happened to leave the brochure open at?"

"Looks good, don't you think?"

"I can't get my head around the idea that there are cruises just for cats."

"Why wouldn't there be?"

"I suppose by now that I shouldn't be surprised at anything. Here, you can have your brochure back."

"Socks is going on that cruise."

"So?"

Socks was Winky's brother. He and I had had a few run-ins. Let's just say, he wasn't on my Christmas card list.

"I thought that maybe you'd like to pay for me to go with him?"

"That's a joke, right?" I laughed. "Have you seen how much it costs?"

"Aren't I worth it?"

"Let me think about that for a minute. Hmm? No."

"You're my human. You're meant to spoil me. That's what other humans do with their cats."

"Spoiling a cat usually involves catnip or cream. It doesn't involve buying passage on a cruise liner. Where do you think I'm going to find that kind of money? Jack and I can barely afford a week in St Annes. What about all the cash you've made from your many money-making ventures?"

"It's all tied up in long term investments."

"You'll just have to untie it then because I'm not forking out for this." I pushed the magazine across to him. "This is why you've been so nice to me lately, isn't it? The cake, the flowers, and the biscuits? You're so transparent."

"And you're ungrateful. Most people would feel blessed to have a feline companion like me. I've been thinking lately that maybe you were never meant to be my human. I've had a few flashbacks from before I was in the human reallocation centre."

"Don't you mean the cat rehoming centre?"

"That man who came in here the other day. What was his name? Carver. He said he'd lost a cat who looked like me. Maybe, he's my human?"

***

Dale Thomas's business partner, Robert Lane, hadn't been keen to talk to me. It had taken many phone calls and much persistence on my part to convince him to spare me some of his time. I finally caught up with him at Washbridge North Airfield where he was tinkering around with an aeroplane, which had a white fuselage and a purple tail.

"I believe that Dale jumped with Skydiving Adventures because your aeroplane was being repaired? Is this the one?"

"It is, and I'll always blame myself for his death."

"Why do you say that?"

"The repair wasn't so urgent that it couldn't have waited a few more days. If we'd taken my plane that day, Dale might still be alive."

"But he blacked out. Surely that could have happened anyway."

"Perhaps, but I keep thinking that if I'd been there, maybe I would have been able to do something. I know that doesn't make any sense, but I can't help it."

"How did Dale seem to you on the days just prior to his death?"

"No different from usual. He had his 'off' days, but then we all do, don't we?"

"He didn't mention anything in particular that was on his mind?"

"No. You're talking as though he committed suicide. That isn't what happened."

"How can you be so sure?"

"Because I knew Dale. He would never have killed himself."

"I've heard it suggested that his wife might have been having an affair. Had he mentioned anything about that to you?"

"Lesley? No. That's ridiculous. Who told you that?"

"It doesn't matter."

"Of course it matters. Who told you Lesley was having an affair?"

"Dale's secretary, Lucy Hannah, said that Dale had mentioned it to her."

"Did she say who Lesley was supposedly seeing?"

"No, Lucy didn't know."

"Of course she didn't know because it's not true. Lucy Hannah had a thing for Dale, but he would never have cheated on Lesley. It strikes me that Hannah is a bitter woman."

"You may be right. I'm sorry, but I have to ask these

questions."

"You're wasting your time. Dale must have blacked out. Nothing else makes any sense."

*　*　*

Although my first priority had to be investigating Dale Thomas's death, I also had to get to the bottom of the problems at Elf Washing machines. If that wasn't resolved quickly, there was a real danger that the retailers in the human world would stop stocking those products. That could be the kiss of death for Elf.

Their factory was one of the larger ones on the Candlefield Industrial Estate. Archie Bald, who had arranged to meet me there, introduced me to Bob Binns.

"Bob has only recently been promoted to factory manager," Archie said. "I'll leave you in his capable hands."

"Pleased to meet you, Jill. What do you need from me?" Binns seemed eager to please.

"Maybe we could start with a quick tour of the factory?"

He obliged, and talked me through the different areas of the production line.

"I have to be honest," I said. "I was surprised to find out that Elves make washing machines."

"I suppose you thought we all made toys?" He grinned. "That's a bit of a stereotype."

"Sorry, I guess so. Do you have any idea what might be causing the current problem, Bob?"

"None. I wish I did. I feel responsible. Archie has shown a great deal of faith in me, and it feels like I'm letting him down."

"Is there anything else you think I should see while I'm here?"

"Just the Quality Control department."

Bob introduced me to Jimmy Underlake, the head of QC. I immediately sensed some kind of friction between the two men.

"You can leave Jill with me, Bob."

"Okay. I'll be in my office if you need me."

After Bob had left us, Jimmy walked me through the QC process. It was very detailed and exceedingly boring.

"So you see, Jill, it's impossible for any machine to leave these premises with a fault. If there was a problem with a machine, we would catch it."

"How do you explain what's been happening recently?"

"I can't. But don't take my word for the rigorousness of our checks. You can test it for yourself."

"What do you mean?"

"When a machine has passed QC, it is sealed in this special packaging. When the machines land at the retailers, that packaging should be undamaged. If it has been tampered with in any way, the stores have instructions to contact us immediately."

"Couldn't someone simply remove the packaging, do the damage, and then repackage it?"

"Impossible. There's no way to duplicate the special packaging materials we use. It would be obvious immediately if someone had done that." He led me to a batch of machines which had passed QC, and were packaged, ready to be dispatched. "Pick any three."

"What do you mean?"

"Pick any three machines you like. We'll remove the

packaging for you to check inside."

I did as he asked—mainly to humour him.

"Take a look at the seals."

They were all in perfect shape.

I left the factory no wiser than when I'd first arrived. Based on what Jimmy had shown me it was hard to see how or where the damage was being done to the washing machines. But, for the sake of Elf, I would have to somehow work it out.

***

When I got back to the office, Alan Carver was waiting for me.

"Alan? I wasn't expecting you, was I?"

"I got a call half an hour ago, asking me to come in."

"Oh?" I glanced at Jules who shook her head. "I'm sorry. I think there's been some kind of mix up."

"Never mind. Look, ever since my last visit, I've been thinking about your cat, Winky. I can't get over how much he looks like my Winky. You don't think I could take another quick look at him, do you?"

"Err—I—err—suppose so. Come on through."

As soon as we walked into my office, Winky began to wrap himself around Carver's legs. His purring was set to maximum volume.

Suddenly, everything made sense. Winky must have used text-to-speech to call Carver and ask him to come into the office.

"Hello again, boy." Carver stroked him. Winky was lapping up all the attention.

"I'm sorry you've had a wasted journey, Alan," I said.

"Don't give it a second thought. It was worth it just to see this handsome boy."

***

We'd just finished dinner. Jack had cooked, so I was doing the washing up.

Jill, have you seen this?" Jack held up a copy of The Bugle.

"What have I told you about that rag? There's nothing in there that could possibly be of interest to me."

"What if I was to say the word 'zombies'?"

Had there been another zombie attack? I'd heard nothing from Z-Watch for some time. It must have been bad if it had made headlines in The Bugle.

"Give it here." I snatched the paper from his hand.

"I thought you weren't interested." He grinned.

"I'm not." I skip read the article, and gave a silent sigh of relief. "It's about a movie."

"What did you think it was? Even The Bugle isn't going to write anything as far-fetched as a story about real zombies."

"This coming from the man who wants to go to PAW meetings."

"That's different. There may well be ghosts or witches living among us, but not zombies."

"I bow to your superior knowledge of the paranormal. Why would they choose Washbridge to shoot their movie? It seems an unlikely choice of location."

"If you read the article, you'll see it's because Washbridge has the highest level of paranormal activity in the country — just like Greg said. They're going to play off that angle when they start to promote the film."

"I hate zombie movies." I handed back the paper.

"I love them. Maybe they'll need some extras."

"You should audition. You wouldn't need much makeup."

"Cheek!" He hit me with the rolled-up newspaper. "If they do audition for extras, we should both go."

"Forget it. I'm not being a zombie for anyone."

Chapter 17

I was in my PJs in the kitchen, munching on toast, and enjoying a nice cup of tea. Outside, it was a beautiful morning—there wasn't a cloud in the sky, the birds were singing, and all was well with the world.

"Jill!" Jack shouted from upstairs. "Did you run off all the hot water?"

I walked to the bottom of the stairs, toast in hand.

"No."

"Are you sure? The water is freezing cold."

"How could I have? I haven't had my shower yet."

"There must be something wrong with the boiler. I'll get dressed and take a look at it."

I ran the hot tap in the kitchen; it was stone cold.

Great!

"It won't come on." Jack had spent the last ten minutes pressing buttons on the boiler.

"What's wrong with it?"

"I don't know. It just won't come on."

"And here was I, thinking that you were a handyman. What am I supposed to do about my shower?"

"Same as I did. Have a cold one. While you're doing that, I'll see if I can find someone to come out to take a look at it."

The water in the shower was absolutely freezing, and by the time I got out, I was blue with cold.

"Did you manage to find someone?" I asked when I got downstairs.

"Eventually, on my tenth call. The others were all booked up for weeks."

"When can he come?"

"That's just it. The only slot he had available was three o' clock this afternoon, and that was only because someone had cancelled. I can't get back here for then because I have a meeting. Can you do it?"

"It doesn't look like I have much choice."

"He goes under the name of Whistle Boilers. Make sure you don't forget, otherwise we're stuffed."

"I'll be here." I couldn't bear the thought of another day with only cold water.

We left the house together.

"Hi, you two." Marco Rollo was walking back up his sister's drive. "I've just been to get a newspaper. Beautiful day, isn't it?"

"Lovely," Jack said. "Hey, we really enjoyed your talk the other night, didn't we, Jill?"

"Yeah." I tried, but failed, to sound enthusiastic.

"Thanks. I thought it went okay."

"I'm thinking of going to more PAW meetings," Jack said.

"You should." Marco was obviously pleased to have made a convert. "What about you, Jill?"

"I don't think so. Not really my thing."

"I was fascinated by the meter that Greg brought along," Jack said. "It's a pity I missed the demonstration. We had to leave because Jill was choking."

Pardon me for almost dying.

"Yeah, I saw you leave. The meter caused a bit of a stir. It actually detected a weak paranormal reading."

"Really?" Jack was way too excited about this.

"Greg said he thought there was some kind of

paranormal activity close to the church hall."

"That's fascinating." Jack turned to me. "Isn't it, Jill?"

"Fascinating."

"Greg allowed me to bring the meter home with me," Marco said. "I could bring it around to your place tonight, if you like. I can show you how it works."

"That would be great." Jack was almost beside himself with excitement. "We could check for paranormal activity in our house."

"What about the boiler repair man?" I said.

"He'll be long gone by then. How's seven o' clock sound, Marco?"

"Sure. I'll come over then."

Oh bum! How was I going to get out of this?

***

After I'd parked the car in Washbridge, I took a walk down the high street to get coffee to-go from Coffee Triangle. En-route, I noticed a camera crew outside a shop four doors down from Ever. The shop had stood empty for some time, but now had a new sign: Top Of The World.

It was Norman's new shop. He might not be a mastermind, but he'd wasted no time in pressing ahead with his new venture. As I got closer, I could see the man himself—he was giving an interview to Toppers TV, who were there to cover the launch.

Although Norman might be the last word when it came to bottle tops, he was an interviewer's worst nightmare. It was obvious that the man with the microphone was struggling to get anything more than monosyllabic responses from Norman.

"Liliana! Liliana! Over here. Could we have a word?"

Only then, did I realise that the man with the microphone was shouting to me. It was the same man who I'd given an interview to when Toppers TV had been on this street before. Liliana Topps was the name I'd made up on the spur of the moment.

"Liliana? It is you, isn't it? Liliana Topps?" The man thrust the microphone under my nose.

"Hi." I engaged my fluffy Liliana voice.

"You must be excited today?"

"Beside myself. I hardly slept last night."

"Did you ever dream that Norman would experience such success?"

"Of course. Why wouldn't he? Norman is the king of the toppers."

"He is indeed. And what will you be buying today, Liliana?"

"I don't know. I can hardly wait to see what opening offers there might be."

"Well, you don't have long to wait because the shop will be opening in, ten, nine, eight…"

The camera was now pointing at Norman who was poised to cut the ribbon. That was my opportunity to get away while everyone was watching Mastermind. A little further up the road, on the opposite side, there was some activity around Betty's shop. She was on the pavement, supervising the three men who were putting her old sign back up. Betty would no doubt be delighted that her shop would once again be known as 'She Sells'.

***

I had decided I should take a look at the location where Dale Thomas had met his end. From what I could ascertain, all Washbridge skydivers, regardless of which of the two airports they flew from, jumped over the same area. The field was about five miles from the south airfield, and about eight miles from the north airfield.

If I'd had any sense, I would have taken a pair of wellies with me. But I didn't, and I hadn't, and my heels kept getting stuck in the mud. What exactly had I expected to find there? There was just a lot of grass. And sheep poo. Thankfully, the offending animals were now in the adjoining field. Sheep and I had a history. Long story—I won't bore you with it.

While I was there, an aeroplane flew overhead, and from it leapt two skydivers. What was the matter with these people? Why would you throw yourself out of a plane, and hope that some huge handkerchief might stop you from plummeting to your death?

This time, their luck held out, and they floated to earth a few hundred yards from where I was standing. As they gathered in their parachutes, and made their way on foot out of the field, I spotted a young boy, sitting on a wooden fence that was the only thing keeping me safe from the killer sheep.

I hobbled slowly over to him.

"You need wellies in these fields," he said.

"I think you're right."

"Have you come to watch them jump?" He pointed to the skydivers.

"No. Is that what you're doing?"

"Yeah. I love to watch them. I want to skydive when I'm

older, but Mum says it's too dangerous."

"I'm Jill. What's your name?"

"Jake Hanby."

"Where do you live, Jake?"

"Over there." He pointed to a farmhouse in the distance. "This is our farm, and those are our sheep. Do you like sheep?"

"Not much. Do you often watch the skydivers, Jake?"

"Yeah."

"Did you know that there was an accident, the other day?"

"Mum told me about it."

"You didn't see it?"

"No."

"Did you see anyone jump that day?"

"Yeah. There were two of them, but they landed okay."

By the time I got back to my car, my feet looked as though they had been dipped in concrete. It took me almost thirty minutes to scrape off all the mud. I was still trying to process what Jake Hanby had told me. He'd said only two skydivers jumped that day, and that they'd both landed safely. That just didn't make sense, but then he was only a kid. Maybe he'd got his days mixed up?

***

Back at the office, Mrs V was knitting, and she was obviously bursting to tell me something.

"They're going to let me train to be a wheelie, Jill."

"Are they? *Wheelie*?"

She gave me that disapproving look of hers.

"Sorry. I couldn't resist. That's good news, I guess."

"It's a great honour. They don't usually consider anyone for training until they've been there for several months."

"Do you have to wear an 'L' plate while you're undergoing training?"

"I don't think you're taking this seriously, Jill."

"I am. I promise. I'm taking it *wheelie* seriously." I hurried through to my office before Mrs V could throw a knitting needle at me.

"Hi, Winky."

He sat up on the sofa, took one look at me, and then turned his back to me.

"Still sulking, then?"

"I can't believe you'd be so mean."

"Because I won't finance your cruise? You can sulk for as long as you like, it isn't happening."

"Meanie!"

"Sticks and stones. How much money do you have squirreled away in all those accounts of yours."

"That's not the point. You're supposed to love me."

I laughed.

Ten minutes later, there was a knock at my office door.

"Come in?"

Mad popped her head inside. "Busy, Jill?"

"Not particularly. Come on in. Isn't Mrs V at her desk?"

"Yeah, she's there, but she said she wasn't speaking to you. What have you done to upset her?"

"I *wheelie* have no idea." I laughed.

"Huh?"

"Never mind. It's nothing. She'll get over it. What can I

do for you? Or is this just a social call?"

"I've been asked to speak to you."

"Oh? By who?"

"My boss, Aubrey Chance."

"The head ghost hunter?"

"His official title is Chief of Law Enforcement, and he wants a meeting with you."

"Why?"

"I don't know. Will you meet with him?"

"Sure, why not? Did he say when?"

"No. I'll have to get back to you."

"Okay."

"You'll never guess what's happened, Jill."

"You've murdered Henry?"

"That's not such a bad idea, but then, knowing him, he'd probably come back and haunt me. No, it's something much more surprising: my mother has thrown Nails out."

"What! They've only been married for five minutes. Has he cheated on her?"

Mad laughed. "Who else would have him?"

"Good point. Has she finally got fed up of his nail clipping?"

"That was my first thought when she told me, but no. It turns out he's an addict."

"Drugs?"

"No, nothing like that."

"Drink?"

"He likes his drink, but so does Mum. It turns out he's addicted to buying bottle tops."

"Really?"

"Is that all you're going to say?" Mad looked surprised.

"I thought you'd think I was pulling your leg. I did, when Mum told me."

"I have some inside knowledge of the murky world of toppers."

"Wow! You must do if you know the jargon. It was all new to me. Mum noticed there was money missing from her weekly shopping stash. She keeps it hidden in the blender."

"Isn't that dangerous? It could get shredded."

"Nah, it hasn't worked for years. Anyway, she realised that it was short, so she confronted Nails. That's when he confessed about the bottle tops. It turns out that a new shop opened in Washbridge recently."

"That would be Norman and Betty's shop."

"Who?"

"They're friends of mine. Kind of. I've got bad news—Norman's just opened an even bigger shop this morning. I was interviewed for Toppers TV about it."

By now, Mad looked thoroughly confused. "Are you into collecting bottle tops, too?"

"Me? No. But Liliana Topps is."

"Who?"

Chapter 18

There was no sign of Amber or Pearl in Cuppy C.

"Where are they?" I asked the assistant who was behind the counter in the tea room.

"Shopping for clothes for their London trip."

"Again? How many do they need for a weekend break?"

She grinned. "You know what they're like."

I did. Poor Alan and William. They would have to ramp up the overtime just to keep up.

"Amber said that if you came in, I should tell you about the new range of muffins."

"Oh?" That was music to my ears. I was always up for trying a new flavour of muffin. "What flavours are they?"

"They're not new flavours. They're the new mini muffins."

"Mini? As in small?"

"Yeah. We have all the usual flavours, but now they're available as mini muffins." She pointed to a tray in the display cabinet.

"Those?" I'd seen bigger crumbs. "And Amber asked you to tell me about them?"

"Yeah. She said you were always asking for a small muffin, so now you can have one."

"I'll keep those in mind, but I'm unusually hungry today, so I think I'll stick to the regular sized ones."

"You mean the giant muffins?"

"Since when were they called 'giant'?"

"Pearl said that from now on we have to ask if customers want a mini or a giant muffin."

"As if anyone would go for the minis." I scoffed at the

idea.

"Actually, most people have. In fact, you're the first person today to ask for a giant one."

Guilt trip or what?

"Really? Okay, well I don't care. I'll stick with the giant muffin. Blueberry, please."

I'd only been there for a few minutes when Daze and Blaze arrived. They bought their drinks and then joined me.

"What are those?" I pointed to Daze's plate.

"A strawberry mini muffin. Blaze has had the black forest mini muffin."

Traitors!

"I see your grandmother managed to talk her way out of trouble with Department V?" Daze took a delicate bite of her strawberry crumb.

"We should have known that she would," I said. "When I tried to warn her about Department V, she seemed completely unconcerned. It turns out the boss over there is an old friend. I should have known."

"Like Teflon, your grandmother. I hear she's introduced yet another one of her 'inventions'?"

"Wi-Fi Needles? Yeah, and from all accounts, they're selling like hot cakes."

"These new muffins are too small," Blaze complained, having finished his in two bites.

"They're perfectly big enough." Daze scolded him. "Only a greedy person would buy the giant ones." She glanced at my plate. "No offence, Jill."

"Hmm? None taken. Hey, Blaze, how are things going with Maze? Is she still seeing that Raze guy?"

"No, she dumped him." He grinned. "We're getting on great, thanks."

"Daze, have you heard of Aubrey Chance?" I asked.

"Of course. He's the head honcho over at the ghost hunters."

"He wants to meet with me, apparently."

"Oh?"

"Mad came to see me to set it up. I've no idea what it's about, though."

"I can guess."

"What?"

"For some time now, there's been talk of finding a witch or wizard who can perform their magic in Ghost Town."

"I didn't think any witch or wizard could go to GT. Other than the dead ones, obviously, and they lose their magical powers when they die. I don't really see the point in it, anyway."

"It's because the criminals over there are getting smarter and smarter. They're always one step ahead of the conventional police. They need someone like you, who has a broad range of magical powers, to outsmart the bad guys. Pretty much like you do here and in the human world."

"That all sounds dandy, but it's meaningless if I can't even travel to GT."

"That's true." She shrugged. "You must let me know what it's all about after you've spoken to him."

"I will, unless he gets me to sign an NDA. What about you two? What are you up to at the moment? Still after Breakskull?"

"He's disappeared off the radar, but I'm sure he'll be back sooner or later—like a bad penny. Right now, we're after a couple of witches who have set up business in Washbridge, offering surgery-free cosmetic surgery."

"Huh? How can cosmetic surgery be surgery-free? That doesn't make sense."

"Perhaps not, but it's an attractive proposition for those who are too scared to go under the knife."

"Are you saying these witches use magic to alter people's bodies?"

"Yep. Scary, isn't it?"

"No kidding. How did you find out about their operation?"

"They made a few mistakes which brought them to our attention."

"Can I tell her the joke?" Blaze interrupted.

"No, you can't!" Daze gave him the 'look'.

"Let him tell me." I was always up for a good joke.

"Alright then, but keep your voice down, Blaze."

He couldn't get it out quickly enough. "The reason we found out about their operation is because they made a few boobs."

Blaze laughed. I laughed. Daze pretended to disown the two of us.

"I needed that," I said, as I wiped tears from my eyes. "I won't be laughing later, though. My neighbour is bringing some kind of paranormal activity meter around to our house tonight."

"I've heard about those things." Daze sounded much too concerned for my liking. "Most of them are phoneys, but I've heard that a few do what it says on the tin."

"This is probably a genuine one. It belongs to PAW."

"I've heard of them too. They take the paranormal business very seriously. What are you going to do?"

"I don't know. I'm really worried."
"I might have an idea."
"Go on. I'm all ears."

***

I called it a day so I'd be back in time for the boiler repair man. I couldn't bear the thought of another day of cold showers.

I'd been in the house for no more than a few minutes when I heard a terrible high pitched noise. At first, I thought it might be Kilbride on his bagpipes, but it seemed to be much closer. And getting louder.

And then it stopped.

There was a knock at the door.

"Is this the Gooder residence?" The man was wearing blue overalls and a blue cap. There was a logo of a whistle on both.

"Whistle Boilers, I assume?"

"The very same. I'm Walter Whistle."

Of course you are.

"Do come in. Do I call you Mr Whistle?"

"No need for formality. Please call me Walt."

"And you must call me Jill."

"What seems to be the problem, Jill?"

"We've had no hot water since this morning."

"We can't have that. Shall I take a look at it?"

"Please. It's upstairs. First door on the left."

"Okey dokey." He started for the stairs.

And then, it began again. The ear-piercing high-pitched whistle. Walter Whistle had the loudest whistle I'd ever heard. My ear drums felt as though they were about to burst. I put my fingers in my ears, but it didn't really help. The noise would have penetrated concrete. I stood it for as long as I could, which wasn't very long, and then went upstairs. Walt already had the boiler stripped down.

"Walt!" I had to shout in order to be heard over his whistling.

"Sorry, Jill. I didn't hear you come upstairs."

I wonder why.

"How's it looking?"

"Not good." He shook his head, and then went on to blind me with all kinds of plumber-speak.

"Can you repair it?"

"Walter Whistle hasn't come across a boiler yet that he couldn't repair."

"That's good."

"It's going to be costly though."

"How costly?"

"Well, there's the parts. And then there's the labour. And the VAT."

"So? Ballpark figure?"

"Two, maybe three."

"Hundred?"

"Thousand."

"What?"

He laughed. "I'm only messing with you. You could get a brand new one for three thousand. I'd say we're looking at three hundred. Ish."

"Could you do it today?"

"I could."

"Great."

"If I had the parts."

"Do you?"

"No. There are so many different makes of boiler. I can't carry parts for them all."

"But you can get them?"

"Of course."

"When?"

"That's the question, isn't it?"

"Yeah. Do you have the answer?"

"I'll need to make a phone call."

"Okay."

He took out his phone. "Johnny? It's Walt Whistle. I've got a Cramshaw 6300. Yeah, I know. Nothing but trouble. The heat exchanger has given up. I know—always the case. Have you got one? —Yeah, I'll hold." He turned to me. "He's checking if he's got one."

"Right." I had my fingers and toes crossed.

"You do? Great." Walt gave me the thumbs up. "Have they? I didn't know that. I'll have to check with my customer." He turned to me again. "Cramshaw put up all their prices a couple of days ago. It's going to be three hundred and fifty now. Is that okay?"

"Sure." Like I had a choice.

"Okay, Johnny. Can you send one over? I'll give you the address."

"Will it be here today?" I asked when he'd finished on the call.

"Oh yeah. Johnny is pretty hot with his deliveries. It should be here within the hour."

"Right. Would you like a drink while you wait?"

"That would be lovely. Tea, please. Milk, no sugar."

As soon as I set off downstairs, he started to whistle again. My nerve-ends were jangling. I'd have to get the tea to him as quickly as I could, and then keep him topped up. He couldn't whistle and drink at the same time. Could he?

***

"Do we have hot water?" Jack asked, as soon as he walked through the door.

"Yes, but I have perforated ear drums."

"Why? What happened?"

"The boiler repair man happened. Walt Whistle's whistle was so loud it almost made my ears bleed."

"You're exaggerating as usual."

"I wish I was. It cost a small fortune too. Three hundred and fifty pounds."

"Still, at least now I can grab a shower before the Rollos come over."

"Can't we cancel? I've had enough paranormal mumbo jumbo to be going on with."

"No, we can't. I'm looking forward to seeing the paranormal activity meter in action. I missed out on it when we were at PAW because of you."

"I'm so sorry for almost choking to death."

I tried a couple more times to persuade Jack that we should cancel on the Rollos, but I was wasting my breath. At seven o' clock, dead on time, Mrs Rollo and Marco appeared on our doorstep.

Mrs Rollo came into the kitchen while I was making drinks for everyone.

"I should have brought some cake with me," she said. "Shall I go back and get some?"

"No!" I said much too quickly. "I mean, there's really no

need. I have lots of biscuits." I opened the cupboard door.

"Custard creams? They're Marco's favourites." She'd spotted the packet I'd tried to hide behind the others.

"His favourites? Great."

"Right then." Marco was in charge of the meter. "Let's see if there's any paranormal activity in this house."

"Go for it!" Jack said.

Marco threw the switch, and immediately the machine began to make a buzzing sound.

"It's detected something." Marco pointed to the various dials on the front of the machine. "Whatever it is must be very close. Maybe even in this room."

Just then, the buzzing got even louder, and the arrows on the dials began to dance around.

"Wait! There's something coming from the kitchen now." He picked up the meter and led the way into the kitchen where my mother's ghost was seated at the table—visible only to me, of course. She gave me a thumbs up.

The buzzing grew even louder, and the dials began to go crazy.

"There's something upstairs!" Marco rushed for the stairs followed closely by Jack and Mrs Rollo.

When I joined them on the landing, Marco was beside himself with excitement.

"They're everywhere!" he yelled. "In here." He pushed open the door to the master bedroom. "And in here." He tried to open the spare bedroom door.

It would only open a few inches, but it was wide enough for me to see a grinning Priscilla. Meanwhile, the colonel popped his head out of the master bedroom.

"Are you sure this thing works?" Jack said. "There can't possibly be paranormal creatures in every room."

"Look at the dials." Marco pointed.

"I think it's pretty obvious that it's a fake," I said.

"I think she's right, Marco." Mrs Rollo nodded.

Marco looked disappointed, but was forced to concede that it was unlikely there would be so much paranormal activity in one house.

"So, do you still believe in all this nonsense?" I asked Jack, after the Rollos had gone home.

"Yes, but I'm not so sure about that meter. I think if we had paranormal creatures in every room, I'd know about it."

Thank you, Daze. That was a brilliant idea!

Chapter 19

I can't tell you how good it felt to have hot water for a shower the next morning. It had almost been worth putting up with Walt and his ear-piercing whistle.

"I've been thinking," Jack said over breakfast.

"Steady on. Is that a good idea?"

"We should have tried that meter back at the Rollo's house to see if it gave a false reading in there too."

"What good would that have done?"

"It would have proven if it was faulty, or if our house is full of paranormal creatures."

"Don't you think we might have noticed something if the house was full of ghosts?"

"I think I'll mention it to Greg when I go to the next PAW meeting. I'd be interested to get his take on it."

"You're serious about going, then? I thought you were joking."

"Deadly serious. I find all this stuff fascinating. I'm surprised you don't."

"I've got better things to do with my time than to chase after imaginary ghosts."

"What would it take to make you believe?"

"More than a machine with lots of dials and a buzzer."

"What if you actually saw a ghost? What then?"

At that precise moment, my mother's ghost appeared behind Jack. She grinned, and waved at me. If she hadn't already been dead, I would have killed her.

"Well?" Jack pressed. "If you actually saw a ghost, would you believe then?"

"Yes, I suppose so, but it's never going to happen."

"We'll see." Jack seemed pleased with that concession.

"I'd better get going." He gave me a toasty kiss.

"What are you playing at, Mum?" I yelled, as soon as Jack was out of the front door.

"Sorry. I couldn't resist."

"It's hard enough trying to maintain my cover without you making it more difficult."

"You're right. I'm sorry. I take it from what I overheard that Jack has developed an interest in the paranormal?"

"An unhealthy interest. He's even talking about going to PAW meetings."

"I wouldn't worry about it. Most of that crowd don't have a clue."

"Most?"

"There are a couple there who are borderline parahumans, but of course they have no idea they are. They could probably sense when a ghost is close by."

"What about a witch?"

"Possibly."

"Great."

***

I'd promised to give Archie Bald an update, so I magicked myself over to Candlefield, and met with him at his house—he hadn't wanted to meet at the factory.

"Lovely home you have here, Archie."

"Thanks, but I can't take any of the credit. Bunty picked it out, and she did all the interior design herself. She was sorry she couldn't be here to meet you—she's a big fan."

"Really?"

"Oh yes. She was rooting for you at the Levels

Competition. She was absolutely livid when the judges disqualified you. We were seated in the bleachers, directly in the path of the dragon that got loose. If you hadn't stopped it, I'm not sure I would have been here to talk to you today. Bunty's at her bridge club, but she asked me to say 'hello' for her."

"I'm afraid I'm not making much progress with the issue you're having, Archie."

"That's really disappointing." He sighed. "Although, not altogether surprising."

"I'm sure I don't need to tell you that none of this makes any sense. The machines appear to be in perfect condition when they're packaged in your QC department, and yet when they're delivered to the customer, still sealed, they appear to have been damaged. I'm struggling to see how or where that damage occurs."

"This is a disaster, Jill."

"Don't despair, yet. There's something else I'd like to try."

"Anything."

"I'd like to install a hidden camera in the QC department."

"Do you think it will do any good? Jimmy told me you picked a few machines at random, and they were all okay."

"That's true. I did. Even so, if I could monitor that department around the clock for a couple of days, then maybe I'll see something. I think it's worth a try."

"Anything is worth a try at this stage. When do you want to install the camera?"

"It will have to be when the factory is empty, obviously. If you could let me have a key, I'll do it tonight."

***

When I arrived back at the office, there was a man waiting for me. I could sense he was a wizard.

"I told this gentleman I didn't know when or if you'd be back, Jill," Jules said. "But he said he wanted to wait."

"Mr?" I approached the man.

"Panny." He stood up. "Please call me Tim."

"Would you like to come through to my office?"

Winky was still sulking.

"How can I help you, Tim?"

"I came to you because I knew you were a witch. This isn't something I could have taken to the police or to a human P.I."

"Okay?"

"I work as a freelance cameraman. Most of my work is in London or abroad. I've never been to Washbridge before. I'm working on 'Zombie Apocalypse', which is being shot up here."

"I read about that in the local paper."

"It's pretty much your average zombie movie. Lots of walking dead running after hapless humans. It's a good gig for me. At least, it was until I realised what was going on." He hesitated. "I suppose that you normally charge people for your services?"

"That's the general idea."

"I thought as much. I can't pay."

I had a bad habit of attracting non-paying clients.

He continued, "The thing is, I'm worried about what's going to happen if something isn't done, and I didn't know who to turn to."

"Why don't you tell me all about it?"

"Okay. I've worked on similar movies to this before. Zombies are very popular at the moment."

Not with me.

"Usually, one of the first things to happen on this kind of movie, is that they recruit a load of extras to be the zombies. That didn't happen."

"How come?"

"Because they're using real ones."

"*Real* zombies?"

"Yeah. The people behind the movie are wizards. From what I can make out, they've paid a gang of body snatchers to get them. It's costing much less than paying extras every day."

"Isn't that dangerous?"

"Very. It's not too bad while they're restricted to the set. They can control them there—although they have to be careful not to let the actors get too close to them. What worries me is if they get out into the general population. That would not be good."

"No kidding." Z-Watch were not equipped to deal with an army of zombies. Before you knew it, they could have turned or killed half of the population of Washbridge. "What are they thinking? They must know how dangerous this is."

"Of course they know, but they don't care. The only thing they're interested in is the bottom line, and this is going to save them a fortune."

"Okay. Leave it with me. I'll sort this."

"Really? I can't pay you."

"I know, but I can't sit back and wait for a real zombie apocalypse, can I?"

Now I knew why Monica and Lester had been having so many problems with body snatchers. The bodies were being taken to the movie set where they were being used as zombies. I had to find a way to stop it.

I made a call.

"Aunt Lucy? It's urgent that I get hold of Monica. Can you contact her through Lester?"

"What do you want her for, Jill?"

"There isn't time to go into detail, but it's a matter of life and death."

"Okay, I'm on it."

***

Despite the looming zombie crisis, I still had to work on the skydiving case. Dale Thomas's brother, Philip, had been conspicuously absent from the funeral. He'd also refused several requests to speak to me. Further requests would have been futile, so I door-stepped him on his way out.

"Philip Thomas?"

"Yes?"

"Could I have a quick word?"

"About what? Who are you?"

"Jill Gooder. I—"

"You're the one who keeps calling me, aren't you? I've already told you that I have nothing to say to you."

I positioned myself between him and his car. He was going to have to go through me.

"This will only take a moment. Don't you want to find out what really happened to your brother?"

"I know what happened. He blacked out, and fell to his death."

"But what if he didn't?"

"Do you have any proof that he didn't?"

"Not yet, but I'm working on it."

"Do you really believe that someone might have killed Dale?"

"I haven't ruled it out."

He took a step back. "Okay, but this had better be quick. There's somewhere I need to be."

"You weren't at your brother's funeral."

"So?"

"The rift between you must have run very deep?"

"Do you think I killed him?"

"No, I'm just trying to get a complete picture of his life."

"Our mother died six years ago. It wasn't pretty at the end. She was in this truly awful care home. I didn't have the money to do anything about it, but Dale did. He wouldn't put his hand in his pocket, so Mum was stuck there until she died. I can never forgive him for that."

"Was he always — err — careful with his money?"

"Careful? Tight-fisted, more like. Yeah, but he got much worse after he married Lesley."

"You're not a fan?"

"I never was. I tried to warn him off her. I told him she was a tramp, but he wouldn't listen. I was proven right though."

"What do you mean?"

"I saw her with that business partner of his."

"Robert Lane?"

"Yeah. They were being a lot more than friendly."

"Did you tell Dale?"

"Why should I after what he did to Mum? He'd made his bed, he could lie in it as far as I was concerned."

"When did you see them together?"

"A couple of months before he died. I was over in West Chipping. I saw them in a pub, laughing and chatting."

"Could they have just been friends out together?"

"No. They were all over each other. I was going to confront them, but then thought better of it. It was nothing to do with me, and no more than Dale deserved."

***

I hadn't long since left Philip Thomas when my phone rang. It was Monica.

"Jill? Lucy said you wanted to speak to me?"

"Where are you?"

"I'm with Lester in Washbridge. What's this all about?"

"Can you both get to Coffee Triangle straight away?"

"We're on duty at the moment. Can't you tell me over the phone?"

"It's better we talk face-to-face. It's about the body snatchers."

"Okay. We'll be there as soon as we can."

Fifteen minutes later, the three of us were seated in Coffee Triangle. Monica and Lester hadn't bothered with anything to eat or drink. I'd got a strawberry muffin (they were out of blueberry), and a latte.

"What do you know about the body snatchers, Jill?" Monica said.

I told them everything I knew about the movie, and the unconventional way they had recruited their zombies.

"They must be insane!" Monica could barely contain her anger. "Don't they realise how dangerous it could be?"

"I doubt they care. They're only interested in the money it will save them. What bothers me—apart from the potential for a mass invasion by zombies—is the poor souls who have been 'snatched'. They should be on their way to Ghost Town or beyond. Not trapped in this world as an extra on a zombie movie. An unpaid extra, at that."

"There may still be time to save them," Monica said.

"How?" I sensed a glimmer of hope.

"Provided they haven't been zombies for more than a month, we can turn them back with Anti-Z formula. The problem is that there are so many of them. How will we ever get to them all?"

"You organise the Anti-Z formula, and I'll do the rest."

Chapter 20

The previous night, when I'd got back from installing a camera to monitor the QC department at Elf Washing Machines, Jack had already been tucked up in bed, fast asleep.

I hadn't bothered with any of those fancy miniature cameras — they were too expensive. Instead, I'd used a cheaper one, but hidden it using the 'hide' spell.

By the time I crawled out of bed the next morning, Jack was long gone. Still, he had left me a love note.

Jill, we're nearly out of toilet paper.

That boy knew how to charm a lady.

It was eight o' clock, and I didn't have time for any breakfast because I'd arranged to meet Monica and Lester at nine. She had phoned late the previous evening to confirm that she'd managed to get her hands on a bumper supply of the Anti-Z formula.

"I don't see how we're going to do this," Monica said when the three of us met in front of my office building. "There must be at least a hundred of them, judging by the figures that we know went missing. You don't expect them to stand in line while we inject them, do you? They'll tear us apart."

"Don't worry. We have a plan." I sounded much more confident than I felt.

I had talked to Daze the night before, to bring her up to speed with the problem. She said she'd come up with something by the morning. I just prayed that she had.

"What are we waiting for?" Monica was clearly getting

jittery. I couldn't blame her.

I glanced down the street. "That's what we're waiting for!"

A flatbed lorry and a small van were heading towards us, and unless I missed my guess, I knew who would be at the wheel.

"Morning, Jill." Daze was driving the lorry. Blaze was driving the van.

"Morning, Daze. Is that going to work?" I pointed to the equipment mounted on the flatbed.

"It will have to. It was all I could come up with at such short notice. Jump in next to me, and get the others to join Blaze."

Monica looked even more worried now, but she and Lester climbed into the cab of the van, alongside Blaze.

"Where are we going?" Daze asked.

I told her where I'd arranged to meet Tim Panny.

If I thought Monica had looked worried, it was nothing compared to how Tim looked when we picked him up.

"What's with all the stuff on the back?" He climbed into the cab alongside me.

"You'll see." Daze didn't bother to introduce herself. "Where exactly are we going?"

"It's about five miles from here." Tim gave Daze directions to the movie set. Blaze followed us in the van.

"Are you sure they'll be in the compound?" I asked.

"Definitely. They never start shooting until eleven at the earliest because they work late into the night.

The perimeter of the movie set was secured by a high wire fence. When Daze pulled up in front of the double gates, Tim jumped out of the cab, and punched in the key code.

We were in.

"The zombies are down there on the right," Tim pointed to a small compound which was enclosed with a similar wire fence.

I'd seen zombies before, but I still wasn't prepared for the sight that greeted us. Dozens of them headed straight to the section of the fence nearest to where we had parked.

"This is awful," Monica said.

She, Lester and Blaze had joined us at the compound fence. Daze was busy using the hydraulic hoist to offload and position the equipment she had brought with her. Twenty minutes later, we were ready to roll.

"Listen up, everyone!" Daze shouted. "This is how it's going to work. When we throw open the compound gates, the Zs will make a rush for it. They'll be funnelled straight into this cage which tapers towards the far end. Over there, at the narrow end of the cage, is a gate that slides back and forth. Blaze, you'll be in charge of that gate. Make sure you only allow one through at a time."

"Roger." Blaze went to take up his position.

What she was describing, resembled the kind of equipment used to control sheep as they waited to be dipped. The idea was that the zombies would move down the narrowing funnel until they were in single file. At that point, they would be allowed to pass through the gate at the far end of the cage, one by one.

"Lester," Daze continued. "Every time Blaze lets a Z through, you need to inject them with the formula. Then, Monica, you need to process them so they can go on their way peacefully."

"But the paperwork takes several minutes."

"Stuff the paperwork. Just fill in the essential parts for now. You can catch up with the rest later."

Neither Monica nor Lester looked very confident, but they both took up their positions.

"What about me?" I said. "What do you want me to do?"

"You and I are here in case something goes wrong. If any Zs get out, we have to stop them."

"How?"

"Improvise."

"Okay." Gulp!

"Right!" Daze shouted. "Tim! On three, release the compound gate. One, two, three!"

As soon as the gate was open, the zombies piled out, and into the cage where they were funnelled into a narrower and narrower space until they were in single file. Blaze slid open the far gate just long enough to allow one through at a time. Lester then injected the poor soul. Thankfully, the formula was quick acting. No sooner had they been injected than they fell to the floor. It was then up to Monica to despatch them as quickly as possible.

It's hard to describe how terrifying the whole process was. I was worried that the sheer volume of zombies in the first part of the cage might prove to be too much, and that the metalwork might give way. If that had happened — I probably wouldn't have lived to tell the tale. Thankfully, the cage held out, and an hour later, the last zombie had been sent on his way.

"Well done, everyone," Daze said.

We were all exhausted, but elated too.

"Come on, Lester." Monica grabbed his arm. "We have

a ton of paperwork to catch up on back at the office."

They had no sooner left with Blaze than a blue BMW came flying down the dirt road towards Daze, Tim and me. Two wizards jumped out.

"What's going on?" The ugliest of the two (and trust me, it was a toss-up) shouted. "Where are the zombies?"

"They've been processed by the grim reapers." Daze stepped forward.

"How dare you? They were our property. We're in the middle of making a movie. We'll sue you."

"Good luck with that." Daze threw a net over the two of them, and they disappeared.

"I guess that means I'm out of a job." Tim shrugged.

"Looks like it," I said. "But you did the right thing."

"I know, but I'm not sure my landlord will agree when I can't make rent. Oh, well. I suppose I'd better start looking for another job."

***

Armi was with Mrs V when I arrived at the office.

"Hi, Armi. Long time no see. How are you?"

"Fine, thanks, Jill. At least I would be if I could talk Annabel into retiring so that we could travel the world together."

"I've told him that you couldn't possibly manage without me, could you, Jill?" Mrs V winked at me.

"It would be difficult, but I'm sure I'd cope. You should go for it, Mrs V."

She gave me a withering look.

"See, Annabel," Armi said. "I told you Jill would understand."

"I'll leave you two to make your plans." I hurried through to my office. Mrs V was so going to kill me.

Winky was on the sofa. Next to him was his suitcase.

"Going somewhere?"

"On that cruise. You know, the one you were too mean to pay for."

"I thought you didn't have any money."

"I've had to cash in some of my long-term investments, which may adversely affect my pension. I hope you can live with yourself."

"I'll try. When are you off?"

"I'm waiting for Socks to come and pick me up."

"He's coming here?"

"Yeah. He should be here at any moment." Winky pointed at the open window.

"Well, I hope you have a good time. Don't forget to bring back a present for me."

"I will, but only if you agree to do me a favour."

"What's that?"

"Can you cover this window with something while I'm away? Black plastic sheeting should do the job."

"Why?"

"I've told Peggy that you're taking me to your family's holiday cottage in the countryside."

"Why did you lie to her?"

"I didn't lie exactly. I was simply being economical with the truth."

"Why not just be honest with her?"

"Because she would have wanted to come too, and I couldn't run to that."

"Is there any wonder your relationships don't last?"

"Will you cover the window or not?"

"No."

"How about you crouch down whenever you go past it?"

Before I could tell him what he could do with his suggestion, the sound of an engine distracted me. Moments later, Socks came sailing through the open window in his microlight.

"Hello, sexy." He flashed that smile of his. "Long time no see."

"Not long enough."

"Still playing hard to get, I see."

Winky grabbed his suitcase, put on a crash helmet, and climbed onto the back of the microlight. "Let's go, bro. Our cruise awaits. See you soon, Jill!"

"Bye."

And with that, they were gone.

***

My phone rang.

"Jill? Are you there?" It was Kathy.

"Yeah, sorry. I was miles away. Have you ever been on a cruise?"

"You know I haven't. Why?"

"No reason."

"What's this all about?"

"Nothing. Someone I know has just gone on one, and I was wondering why I couldn't afford to."

"If you cut back on custard creams, you probably could."

"Don't be ridiculous. Oh, well, I'd better get going."

"Hold on! It was me who rang you, remember?"

"Oh yeah. Sorry."

"Pete is taking Mikey fishing on Saturday."

"Has he been misbehaving? Is that some kind of punishment?"

"No. Mikey wants to go."

Weird kid.

"Anyway," Kathy said. "Lizzie and I are going to The Central, and we wondered if you'd like to come?"

"What for?"

"Not *for* anything. Just for fun."

"Fun? In a mall?"

"I can see this was a mistake. Don't worry. I'll tell your niece you don't want to go with us."

"Wait. Don't do that. How long would it be for?"

"Three or four hours. We can get a coffee and something to eat."

"Okay then. Jack said he was bowling this weekend, anyway."

"Great. I'll give you a call later to arrange a time."

When I'd finished on the call, I realised that Mrs V was standing in the doorway to my office — glaring at me.

"Hi." I smiled, for all the good that was going to do.

"You and I need to have words, Jill."

"I was just about to look at my balance sheet."

"You don't even know what one of those is." She approached my desk like a lion stalking its prey.

"I was only joking about the retirement thing." I managed a weak laugh.

"I'd just about persuaded Armi that his idea to travel the world was a non-starter, and then you go and stir it all up again with your little joke."

"Sorry." I whimpered.

"The next time Armi asks if it would be okay for me to retire, and if you'd be able to cope without me, what will you say?"

"That I couldn't possibly manage without you?"

"Correct."

Chapter 21

Dale Thomas's brother, Philip, had never forgiven him for refusing to provide additional funding to improve the care of their mother in her final days. Was Philip's accusation that Lesley Thomas had been having an affair with Robert Lane true, or a lie fuelled by his animosity towards his brother? I had to find out.

I'd tried without success to get hold of either Lesley Thomas or Robert Lane. Neither of them was returning my calls, so I tried a different tack. I called Robert Lane's office to try to make an appointment under some fictitious name, on the pretence that my company may have work that it was considering putting Lane's way. The PA who answered told me that Lane wasn't in, and when pressed, confirmed he was working on his aeroplane, and wouldn't be in until the following day.

It was time to pay another visit to Washbridge North Airfield.

"You again?" Lane was clearly pleased to see me. "What do you want?"

"I've called you several times and left messages, but you didn't return my calls."

"Maybe that should have told you something? Why don't you let Dale rest in peace?"

"How long have you and Lesley been having an affair?"

Subtle, that's me.

"That's nonsense. Lesley and I are friends—nothing more than that."

"You were seen in West Chipping being much more than friendly with one another."

His face flushed red, whether from embarrassment or

anger, I couldn't be sure.

"Who saw us? Who told you that?"

"Dale's brother."

"Philip?" He scoffed. "You can't believe anything he says. He hated Dale."

"Dale's gone now. What would Philip have to gain by lying?"

"Who knows how he thinks? He isn't right in the head. Look, I'm telling you that there's nothing going on between Lesley and me. There never has been. I'd like you to leave now."

Lane went back to working on his plane.

I wasn't sure what to make of his reaction. Had he been outraged at hearing an unfounded accusation, or concerned that I knew the truth? If he and Lesley had been having an affair, that might be a motive to get rid of Dale, but it still left a very big question.

How?

***

Mad had been in touch to set up a meeting between me and her boss, Aubrey Chase. He'd asked that we meet in Washbridge Park, on the bench closest to the bowling green—all very cloak and dagger. I'd asked Mad if I needed some kind of secret pass phrase like: *the fleas are biting today* or *pork chops are half price in the precinct*.

Mad had said I didn't, but that I'd know her boss because he'd be wearing a grey suit. It might have been more helpful if she'd mentioned he had only one arm.

"Jill?" He offered his hand. His left hand. As I normally

shake with my right, that made the whole handshake thing a little awkward.

"Thanks for agreeing to this." He took a seat next to me on the bench.

"No problem. Mad's a good friend."

"And an excellent operative." He grinned. "Even if she can be a little wilful at times."

"She didn't tell me what this was about."

"No. I wanted to do that face to face. You may already have heard that there's been a dramatic increase in the amount of ghost activity in and around Washbridge?"

"Yes, I have heard a few reports."

"In itself, that's not a cause for concern, but it has occurred during a corresponding increase in crime rates in GT."

"Do you have any theories why that is?"

"More than just theories. We know that certain sections of the sup criminal community have realised there's potential for profit in GT. It's becoming more and more difficult for sups to run their criminal enterprises in the human world because the rogue retrievers are now much more effective at closing them down. So instead, the criminals are now partnering with ghosts, in order to expand their operations into GT."

"And you have evidence that this is happening?"

"Yes, and it's getting worse all the time."

"I'm still not sure where I come in?"

"Our police force is doing a magnificent job, but they can only do so much. We need someone with magical powers to combat the worst offenders. A powerful wizard or witch."

"I don't see how that's ever going to happen because

sups can't travel to GT."

"You may be the exception."

"Why on earth would you think that?"

"There are rumours that one particular sup was able to do it. A witch by the name of Magna Mondale. I believe you will have heard of her?"

"Of course, but you said 'rumours'. I take it you don't have any proof that she was able to do this?"

"No."

"Which means it may not be true?"

"But it might be, and that's why I wanted to speak to you. I've done a lot of research into your background, and it's clear to me that you have some kind of connection with Magna Mondale."

"Not really. I was able to get into her sealed room, and I had her book for a short while. That's all."

"Maybe. But you must have asked yourself: *why you?*"

"Not really," I lied.

"Would you be prepared to give it a try?"

"What would I need to do?"

"If you agree, I'll ask Mad to liaise with you. Her parahuman powers are part of her being, but maybe they can be emulated by your extraordinary magical powers."

"I don't see how."

"What do we have to lose? Would you at least be prepared to try?"

"Sure."

"That's great." He stood up. "I'll brief Mad, and ask her to contact you."

Although I liked the idea of being able to travel to GT, I didn't hold out much hope of it ever happening. There was no precedent for it other than some rumours that Magna Mondale may have been able to do it.

Interesting times!

***

"You're quiet," Jack said.

We were supposedly watching TV, but I had drifted away with thoughts of zombies and ghosts.

"Sorry. I'm just tired. I shuffled lots of paper today."

"Are you ever going to let me forget that?"

"Probably not. How was your day?"

"Busy. They're going to have to bring in some extra bodies soon just to keep pace."

It was a sign of the unusual life which I led that when Jack said 'bodies', I immediately pictured zombies.

"Kathy has asked me to go to the new mall with her and Lizzie on Saturday."

"Did you say you'd go?"

"Yeah, but now I'm wondering if I should call and cancel."

"If you decide not to go, you could always cut the hedge. It's getting a little long."

"Come to think of it, I probably should go to the mall. I don't get too many chances to spend time with my niece."

Just then, a howling noise came from somewhere behind the house.

"What was that?" Jack stood up. "It sounded like a wolf."

"Don't be ridiculous. There aren't any wolves In Washbridge. It was probably just a dog."

Despite what I'd said, there was no doubt in my mind —

that wasn't a dog. When Jack had said 'wolf', he'd been close, but that wasn't the sound of a regular wolf. That was unmistakably the howl of a werewolf.

"I think I'll take a short stroll." I stood up.

"I thought you were beat?"

"It might wake me up."

"I'll come with you, if you like?"

"No. You stay here and watch—err—what is that rubbish you're watching?"

"It's Celebrity Candle Makers."

"Right. I won't be long." I was out of the room before he had time to object.

I hurried down the back garden, and scrambled over the fence into the fields. There had only been the single howl, but I was fairly sure I knew from which direction it had come. I could think of no reason why a werewolf would be hanging around there. Even more confusing was why it would draw attention to itself by howling. It would have made more sense if it had been a full moon, but that wouldn't be for several days.

Another howl. It seemed to be coming from a patch of bushes a few yards to my right. I'd have to be careful; an angry werewolf could be a handful.

As I neared the bushes, I spotted a very small, very young werewolf.

"What are you doing?" I shouted.

I'd obviously made him jump because he backed away, and bared his teeth.

"You have to change back to human form before someone sees you."

The wolf didn't move for the longest moment, but then shifted into human form. The young boy grabbed the clothes that he'd obviously discarded earlier.

"Get dressed, quickly." I turned my back on him while he did. "What are you doing here?"

"I've lost my dad."

"Where did you last see him?"

"I don't know." He looked around. "It was a long way away. In a town. I went to look in a shop, but he'd gone when I came out. I couldn't find him anywhere."

"How did you end up here?"

"I just ran and ran. I thought if I ran far enough I might get back home."

"Do you live in Washbridge?"

"No, in Candlefield. This is my first trip to the human world. It's a bit scary."

"You're not afraid of me, are you?"

"No." He didn't look too sure. "You're a witch, aren't you?"

"Yeah. You can't stay here. It's too dangerous. You'd better come back to my house, and we'll find your dad in the morning."

"Okay."

"What's your name?"

"Conrad."

"Look, Conrad, there's something you need to know. The man I live with, Jack, is a human. He doesn't know I'm a witch, and he mustn't know you're a werewolf."

The boy nodded.

"No shifting. Understood?"

"Okay."

"Look who I've found." I was back in the house. Conrad was holding my hand.

"Who's this?" Jack gave me a quizzical look.

"I found him wandering the streets. He's lost his dad."

"Oh dear. Don't worry, young man. I'm a policeman. I'll call my colleagues, and they'll — "

"No!" I snapped. "That's not necessary."

"Why ever not? His parents will be crazy with worry."

"I've spoken to them already," I lied. "I told them he's safe. His father is going to come and collect him in the morning."

"And they were okay with that?"

"Yeah. They were just relieved to know he's alright."

"Fair enough."

"He can sleep on the sofa, but first I'll make him something to eat. He must be starving."

After Conrad had finished his supper, Jack and I decided to call it a day. Jack went up first.

"Will you be okay down here?" I put a blanket over the young boy.

"Yes, thanks. Have you really spoken to my dad?"

"No, but I didn't want Jack to call the police. Don't worry, we'll find your dad first thing tomorrow. Now, try to get some sleep."

"Okay. Goodnight."

Chapter 22

It had taken me a while to get off to sleep because I'd half expected Conrad to call out, but he'd been as quiet as a lamb, or at least a lamb in wolf's clothing.

"Do you think we should go down and check on him?" Jack nudged me awake the next morning.

"Leave me alone. I'm asleep."

"It's gone seven."

"Already? Are you sure?"

"Yes. Come on. What time did his dad say he was coming to collect him?"

"He couldn't get here until after nine. You go to work as normal. I'll wait in for him to arrive."

"Are you sure? I don't mind waiting with you."

"That's not necessary. And besides, you said you had a lot on. I'll be fine."

I led the way downstairs. There was no sign of Conrad on the sofa, but then I spotted him curled up under the table.

In wolf form.

"Wait there!" I slammed the lounge door in Jack's face.

"Jill? What's going on?" Jack shouted.

"Nothing. If Conrad wakes up and finds you looking down at him, he might be scared." I turned to the young wolf. "Conrad! Wake up! Conrad!"

"Why would he be scared of me?" Jack tried to push the door open, but I'd cast the 'power' spell so I was able to keep it closed.

"You haven't had a shave. You look scary with your stubble." I managed to tap the wolf with my foot.

"Conrad! Wake up!"

The wolf stirred, and got to his feet.

"You have to shift back into human form," I said, in a hushed voice.

Jack pushed at the door again.

As soon as Conrad had shifted back into human form, and put on his clothes, I let Jack in.

"What was that all about?" Jack gave me a puzzled look.

"Conrad was a little disorientated when he woke up, but he's okay now, aren't you?"

The young boy nodded.

"Would you like some breakfast?"

Before the boy could answer, there was a loud knock at the door.

"Who's that at this time?" Jack started for the door.

"Wait!" I had a horrible feeling I knew who it would be, but I was too slow to stop Jack.

The man at the door was an enormous werewolf, in human form. "You've taken my son, human!"

Oh bum!

"I didn't think you were coming until after nine," Jack said.

"I'm going to tear your throat out." The man reached out to grab Jack.

I had to act quickly, so I used the 'faster' spell to get between Jack and his assailant. After casting a 'freeze' spell on Jack, I cast the 'power' spell to allow me to hold back the werewolf.

"Get out of my way!" He growled.

"Wait! Conrad is safe."

"Why did this human take him?"

"No one took him. He was lost. I found him in the fields behind our house. Where were you? Why did you leave him alone?"

"I didn't. I turned my back for a few seconds, and he'd gone. I've been tracking him all night. Is he really okay?"

"He's fine. Come through — he's in here."

"Conrad!" He picked up the boy and held him tight. "Why did you wander off? I've been really worried."

"Sorry, Dad. I didn't mean to."

"It doesn't matter. You're okay, that's all I care about."

The werewolf's name was Simon Small (ironic, I know). He refused my offer of a cup of tea because he wanted to get his son back to Candlefield.

"Thank you again," he said, as they were leaving. "And I'm sorry for what I said to the human."

"That's okay. I'll sort it."

I reversed the 'freeze' spell, and quickly cast the 'forget' spell.

"Where's the boy gone?" Jack looked around.

"His dad came early to collect him."

"He did? How come I didn't see him?"

"You were in the loo."

"Oh? Right. I must still be half asleep."

***

Jules was knitting a hat/sock/something unrecognisable.

"Morning, Jill. The weirdest thing happened last night. You'll never guess what."

"A werewolf slept on your sofa?"

"Huh? No. I found a lipstick that I lost last year."

"That is weird."

"I rang Gilbert to tell him."

"Right."

"He thought it was weird too."

But not half as weird as this conversation.

"Hey, Jill, did you know they're making a zombie movie, right here in Washbridge?"

"I did hear something about it."

"It's great, isn't it? I love zombie movies, even though they make me jump. I can't wait to see it."

"You might be waiting a while. I hear they ran into some difficulties."

The office always seemed empty when Winky wasn't there. He might have driven me insane most of the time, but I kind of missed him in a sort of masochistic way.

"Jill? Why are you stooping down like that?" Jules had followed me into my office.

"Err—I—err dropped something." I could hardly tell her that I was trying to avoid being seen by the cat from across the way, could I?

"What did you drop? I'll help you look for it."

"It was a—err—paperclip."

"I've got plenty more in my desk."

"It's my favourite one."

"You have a favourite paperclip?"

"Was there something you wanted, Jules?"

"I was wondering if I could have a day's holiday on Wednesday next week?"

"Couldn't you just swap days with Mrs V?"

"I'll ask her, but she seems rather busy with that wheelie mealie thing."

"Did you want to do something in particular next Wednesday?"

"Me and Gilbert are going on the BP Getaway."

"BP?"

"Black Pudding. It's where I used to work, remember?"

"Of course." How could I forget?

"I'm still in touch with the people there. They have a Getaway Day every year. It's Skegness this year."

"Okay. Well, if Mrs V can't swap, you can still take the day off."

"Thanks, Jill. I'll bring you back a stick of rock."

I spent the best part of the next hour going over all my notes on the Dale Thomas death. Had Robert Lane been having an affair with Dale's wife? I only had Philip Thomas's word for that. If it was true, it might have given one or both of them a motive to get rid of Dale. All of that seemed irrelevant, though, because Gerry Southland had been adamant that Dale had been conscious and in good health when he'd jumped from the plane.

I reread the notes I'd made after speaking to Jake Hanby, the young boy who lived at the farmhouse close to the drop site. He'd said he hadn't seen the fall, but he had seen two skydivers land safely. I hadn't thought much of it at the time because I'd assumed he must have seen two other skydivers. But, before I told Carver that there was no evidence of foul play, I decided to have another chat with the young boy — just to be sure.

Before I went to speak to Jake, I wanted to look through the recording that I'd made of the QC department at Elf Washing Machines. The camera, which I'd hidden there, was saving images to the 'cloud', which I could access directly from my computer.

Come on, be honest. You're impressed with my computer savvy, aren't you? Oh, alright, I admit it. I paid someone to set it up, so all I had to do was plant the camera.

I fast forwarded through hours of footage, which was almost as boring as Celebrity Candle Makers. There was nothing to see. Every washing machine went through the same thorough checks, and was then sealed ready for shipment. The only people captured on the footage were Jimmy Underlake and his staff.

Another dead end.

Both of the cases I was working on were headed nowhere fast.

"Jill!" Jules stepped into my office, and pulled the door closed behind her. "There's a young woman who'd like to see you."

I'd been about to go and see Jake Hanby, but a few more minutes wouldn't make any difference.

"Okay. Show her in, would you?"

"There's something I should warn you about."

"What's that?"

"Her hat. It's strange — really strange."

"Okay, thanks. Consider me forewarned."

The woman's hat *was* indeed strange, but I knew why she was wearing it. She was an elf, and the hat was to hide her ears, which were a bit of a giveaway in the human world.

"Thanks for seeing me. I'm Lola Bodmore." She took a seat, and then removed her hat. "I'm glad to get that off.

My ears are burning."

"What can I do for you, Lola?"

"I believe you're investigating the problems over at Elf Washing Machines?"

"I am, yes."

"I work there in R&D. I've been there for six years now."

"Do you know what's been causing the issues with the washing machines?"

"No, I don't."

"So, why *are* you here?"

"I'm worried about Bob Binns. He and I started at Elf around the same time. I'm concerned that he may end up carrying the can for this."

"Are you saying he may be responsible for the damage?"

"Good gracious, no. He would never do anything like that. Bob has more integrity than anyone I know. I just think he'll be blamed because these problems started on his watch."

"I see."

"Did you know that Jimmy Underlake was passed over for the position of factory manager?"

"I didn't."

"Jimmy has been there much longer, but Archie thought Bob was the better candidate. And he was right. Jimmy is too full of himself."

"Are you suggesting that Underlake may be behind this? That he's trying to get Bob Binns sacked?"

"I have no proof, but yes."

"It isn't much to go on."

"I know." She stood up, and put on her hat. "I'm sorry

if I've wasted your time. I just felt I had to try to help Bob."

***

I'd expected to have to go to the farmhouse to talk to Jake Hanby, but I found him sitting on the same wooden fence as before.

"Hi!" I called to him. "Watching for skydivers, again?"

"Yeah. There haven't been any today, though."

I climbed onto the fence next to him.

"When I spoke to you last time, you mentioned that you saw two skydivers land on the day of the accident."

"Yeah, I did."

"How many others did you see jump that day?"

"They were the only ones."

"Maybe there were some other skydivers before you came out or after you went back home."

"There weren't."

"You seem very sure."

"I am. I came out as soon as it was light, and I brought a packed lunch with me so I didn't have to go back to the house. When I needed to—err—you know—I went behind that tree. I didn't go back home until it was starting to go dark. They never jump after dark."

"I believe you, but isn't it possible that you only saw one parachute open?"

"No!" He looked most indignant. "I know how to count to two!"

"Sorry, yes, of course. Just so I'm absolutely clear, that was the only aeroplane that came over that day?"

"I didn't say that. I said there weren't any more

skydivers."

"But there was another plane?"

"Yeah."

"Was that before or after the one with the skydivers in it?"

"Before. It was really early—it was only just light. I heard it go over, and had to hurry out of the house to see it."

"And did you?"

"Yeah. In the distance."

"But there were no skydivers?"

"No, or I would have seen their parachutes."

"Had you seen that plane before?"

"Yeah. Lots of times. But there's always been jumpers before."

"Can you describe that first plane? What colour was it?"

"White with a purple tail."

Chapter 23

For the first time since I'd started work on the Thomas case, I had a lead, or at least the makings of one. To confirm my suspicions, I wanted to speak to Gerry Southland again. Before I did, I needed to get hold of the photograph that Alan Carver had shown me when he'd first visited my offices. I called him, and asked him to email me a copy. He pressed me to tell him why I wanted it, but I managed to stall him with a promise that I'd update him as soon as I could.

"Hello, again," Gerry Southland was cleaning his plane with a jet wash. "Whoops, sorry!"

When he'd turned around to greet me, he'd failed to switch off the jet wash straight away; I was soaked to the skin.

"That's okay. I'll dry." Eventually.

"Are you still investigating the Thomas death?"

"Just clearing up a few loose ends before I report back. Would you take a quick look at this photograph?" I took out my phone, and pulled up the photo which Carver had sent to me. "Can you confirm that these are the two people that you took skydiving that day?"

Gerry took my phone, and studied the image. "Yeah. That's Mrs Thomas, and that guy is Mr Thomas."

"You're sure about that?"

"Positive. Why?"

"No reason." I took my phone back. "I just wanted to be absolutely sure."

***

I was now convinced that Dale Thomas's death had not been an accident or suicide. He had been murdered, but proving it wasn't going to be easy. What I needed was a confession, but to get that I was going to have to resort to magic.

Once I was outside of Lesley Thomas's front door, I used a burner phone to make an anonymous call to Washbridge police station. The officer who took the call asked several times for my name, but I ignored him, and insisted he passed the message to Leo Riley straight away. The clock was now running, so this had to work, or I would be in deep doo doo.

I cast the 'doppelganger' spell, and knocked on the door.

"Dale?" Lesley screamed, and her legs buckled, but I managed to catch her before she hit the deck.

"Let me help you inside, my sweet." I put her arm over my shoulder, pushed the door closed with my foot, and then led her into the lounge, where I lowered her gently onto the sofa.

Her eyes were wide, and her mouth was open, but she didn't speak for several minutes. Eventually, she managed, "Dale?"

"Surprised to see me, dear?"

"It can't be you."

"I'm pretty sure it is."

"This is a dream." She began to cry. "It's just a bad dream."

I touched her hand. "Does that feel like a dream?"

She pulled her hand away. "Go away! Go away!"

"Not until you tell me why you did it."

"It wasn't my idea. It was Bob's."

"But you went along with it?"

"I'm sorry."

"You knew when Robert and I left that day that he was going to kill me, didn't you?"

"I saw you buried."

"Didn't you, Lesley?"

"Yes, yes, I knew, but he said there was no other way."

"So, after he'd knocked me out and pushed me from his plane, you and he jumped from Southland's aeroplane. And Robert pretended to be me. That's what happened, isn't it?"

"Yes, but it wasn't my idea. I wanted to get a divorce, but Bob said it would take too long, and that I'd lose all the money. It was all his idea. I'm sorry."

Right on cue, there was a loud knock at the door.

"Mrs Thomas? It's the police. Please open the door!"

Lesley Thomas was in no condition to do anything, so I quickly reversed the 'doppelganger' spell, and then answered the door.

Riley's face was a picture.

"Gooder? What are you doing here? Was it you who called us?"

"Me? No. I was just interviewing Mrs Thomas. She's decided to come clean. It seems that Robert Lane killed Dale. He must have knocked him unconscious and thrown him out of his plane. Then Lesley and Robert jumped from Gerry Southland's plane. Robert Lane pretended to be Dale Thomas. If you talk to her, I'm sure she'll fill you in on all the details. Anyway, I have to be going."

I tried to sidestep him, but he blocked my way.

"You're not going anywhere. Officer, take this woman back to the station."

There was no point in arguing, so I allowed the officer to put me in the back of the police car, and take me to my favourite holding cell. By now, I knew every square inch of that small room, including all the graffiti, some of which made for interesting reading.

"Detective Riley will see you now." A female officer escorted me to the interview room where my best friend was already seated.

"That cell could really do with a lick of paint."

"Keep quiet, Gooder."

"Isn't that going to make this interview rather difficult?"

"You made an anonymous call to the station, didn't you? I've just listened to the recording. I know it was you."

"No, I didn't." I'd used magic to disguise my voice, so I knew he was bluffing.

"Are you seriously trying to tell me that you went to Lesley Thomas's house to interview her, and she suddenly broke down and confessed everything?"

"Pretty much, yeah."

"I don't buy it. She's been ranting about her husband coming back to haunt her."

"She thinks she's seen a ghost?"

"Did you pretend to be her husband?"

"Do I look like Dale Thomas?"

"Did you drug her?"

"Now you're just being ridiculous. Why don't you give her a blood test?"

"Ever since I moved here, you've been a thorn in my side, and I'm getting pretty fed up with it."

"How am I being a thorn in your side, when all I'm doing is solving your cases for you?"

His face was so red, I half expected his head to explode.

"I don't need your help. I just want you to stay out of my way. My life is difficult enough as it is."

"Really? I always thought you had the life of Riley." I laughed.

He didn't.

***

Lola Bodmore's visit to my office had got me thinking. Was it possible that Jimmy Underlake was sabotaging the washing machines in the hope that Bob Binns would lose his job as factory manager? Underlake apparently thought the job should have been his. The problem was I'd seen the QC process at first hand, I'd examined a number of machines at random, and I'd seen the footage from the camera. There was zero evidence so far to support the idea that he was behind the sabotage.

There was one last thing I wanted to try. If nothing came of it, I'd have to tell Archie Bald that I'd drawn a blank. When I'd spoken to Underlake in the factory, he'd been relaxed and confident. Maybe, if I turned up at his home unannounced, I'd catch him off guard. I wanted to question him about his discontent at being overlooked for the factory manager's job.

Underlake lived in the area known as Elf Central. That wasn't its official name, but the locals called it that because of the large number of elves who had chosen to take up residence there. Underlake lived at thirty-seven Elfin Drive—a small terraced property. The front garden was an eyesore, which can't have gone down well with his neighbours on either side, both of whom had beautifully maintained gardens.

"What do you want?" Underlake was clearly surprised to see me.

"Can I have a quick word?"

"What about?"

"Can I come in? It should only take a few minutes."

"Can't we do this at the factory?"

"I have to report back to Archie Bald this evening," I lied. "I suppose I could tell him you wouldn't speak to me."

"There's no need for that." He stepped aside.

Once inside, I reached for the handle of the first door.

"Not in there!" He grabbed my hand. "Sorry, err—I've just decorated. The paint is still wet."

I couldn't smell paint, but there was another smell—a strange one that I couldn't place.

He led the way to a room at the back of the house that overlooked a garden, which was even more untidy than the one on the front. It didn't help that there was a pile of tyres in the middle of the unkempt lawn. That explained the strange smell—I realised then that it was rubber.

"Why are you here?" he snapped. My visit had clearly rattled him for some reason. "I've already told you everything I know."

"Yes, and I'm grateful. I just have one more question for you. How did you feel when Archie gave the factory manager's job to Bob Binns instead of you?"

He shrugged. "It didn't bother me."

"Are you sure about that? From what I heard, you thought the job was yours."

"It should have been," he snapped again. "But it was Archie's decision."

"What do you think of Bob Binns?"

"What does it matter what I think about him?"

"Do you think he's doing a good job?"

"It's none of my business." He made a point of checking his watch. "Look, I have to go out soon. Have we done?"

"Do you think the current problems are down to Binns?"

"He's the factory manager, isn't he?"

"Do you think he should lose his job over this?"

"Like I said. It's down to Archie. Now, if you wouldn't mind?"

He ushered me out of the door.

That had been an interesting encounter. Underlake certainly hadn't acted like a man with nothing to hide. He'd been nervous and evasive, and when I'd mentioned his being overlooked for the factory manager's job, I'd obviously hit a raw nerve. And why had he stopped me from going in the front room? He'd said that he'd just decorated, but I couldn't smell paint.

There was something fishy going on, and it warranted another look.

**

"Aren't you coming to bed?" Jack said, just after eleven o' clock.

"I have to go out."

"Why?"

"It's a case I'm working on."

"How come you didn't mention it earlier?"

"I didn't want you to worry." Ever since I'd been kidnapped by crazy Elsie, Jack had had a tendency to panic whenever I had to work late.

"What's the case?"

"Industrial sabotage."

"What will you be doing?"

"What is this, twenty questions?"

"I just don't want you to get hurt."

"I thought we'd agreed that you wouldn't give me a hard time over my work."

"I know, but I still worry."

"Aw. That's sweet." I gave him a peck on the lips. "I can look after myself. You should know that by now."

"Be careful."

***

There were no lights on in Jimmy Underlake's house. That was a good sign. It was dark, and there was no one on the street, so I used the 'shrink', 'levitate' and 'power' spells to gain access to the house via the letterbox. The smell of rubber was even stronger, and it seemed to be coming from the front room, the one which Jimmy had stopped me entering.

Back to full size, I turned the handle on the door. It wasn't locked. Inside, the smell was overpowering, and I could see why. On the table was a glass dome, under which were the remains of what looked like a small section of a tyre.

What was going on? Why would Underlake have a pile of old tyres in his back garden, and a section of tyre under a glass dome? I edged my way closer, so I could get a better look at the contents of the glass dome.

And then, I spotted them.

Chapter 24

"You're here?" Jack said when he woke the next morning, and found me beside him in bed.

"Who else were you expecting?"

He stretched. "What time did you get back?"

"I wasn't too late."

As soon as I'd found what I was looking for, I'd left Jimmy Underlake's house the same way as I'd gone in.

"I didn't hear you come in."

"I'm not surprised, the way you were snoring."

"I don't snore."

"Of course you don't. And I don't like custard creams."

"Was it a success? Your top secret late night mission?"

"Enough of the questions. I can think of much better things you could be doing."

"Oh?" He grinned, and seemed suddenly much more awake. "What did you have in mind?"

"Go and make me a cup of tea and some toast."

***

"What are you doing, Jill?" Mrs V had caught me stooping below the window. Why was I trying to save Winky's love life from imploding again? I was a slave to that feline.

"I — err — dropped something."

"What?"

"Err — a rubber band."

"There's plenty more in the cupboard."

"It was my favourite one."

"You have a favourite rubber band?"

"Did you want something, Mrs V?"

"Mr Carver is out there. Do you have time to see him, or shall I tell him that you're too busy looking for your favourite rubber band?"

"Send him in, please."

"Jill, thank you for seeing me without an appointment." Alan Carver was all smiles.

"No problem. Have a seat."

"I just wanted to come over and thank you. They've arrested Lesley and Robert, but I suppose you already know that."

"Yes. They'll probably both be charged with murder, even though it was Robert who actually killed Dale."

"I still don't understand how they did it."

"It was Lesley and Robert who jumped from Skydiving Adventure's aeroplane. Robert was posing as Dale. Gerry Southland had never seen any of them before, so there was no reason to question the names they gave. They were seen making a safe landing by a young boy who lived close to the drop zone. He was the one who alerted me to the fact that another aeroplane had passed over earlier that day. That had been Robert's plane. Lane must have somehow persuaded Dale to jump solo that day. Lesley must have cried off—perhaps she said she wasn't feeling well—who knows? Lane knocked Dale out, and then pushed him from the aeroplane. By the time Robert and Lesley made their jump, Dale was already on the ground—dead. Robert made his escape while Lesley raised the alarm."

"Did the young boy see Dale fall to his death?"

"Thankfully, no. He heard Lane's plane go over, but by

the time he got out of the house, it was already in the distance. He looked for parachutes, but there were none."

"I don't understand how you managed to get Lesley to confess."

"I didn't do anything, really. I think the guilt must have got to her in the end."

"I can't thank you enough, Jill. None of this will bring Dale back, but at least his murderers will be brought to justice. Do you have your bill ready?"

"Not at the moment, but I'll put it in the post tonight."

He was about to leave, but then hesitated. "I almost forgot. I have something to show you." He took out his phone. "This is a photo of my Winky."

Oh bum! If *his* Winky turned out to be *my* Winky, how could I continue to lie to Carver. I'd have to admit I got my Winky from a rehoming centre, and offer to hand him back.

"There you go." He held out the phone.

"He's a handsome cat." I smiled. "And very similar in appearance to my Winky, except for one thing."

"Oh?"

"It's the wrong eye."

"Sorry?"

"They both have a missing eye, but not the same one."

"Really?" He glanced around the office. "Where is the handsome boy?"

"He's gone on a—err—I mean—err—he's on holiday."

"Without you?"

"My cousin has taken him. She's very fond of Winky."

"I see. Oh, well, thanks again, Jill."

Phew! My Winky actually was *my* Winky!

Why was I so pleased?

***

"Have you found your favourite rubber band, yet, Jill?" Mrs V was never going to let this one go.

"Yes, thanks."

"Your accountant, Mr Stone, is here. Can you see him?"

"Yes, please send him through."

"Luther? Whatever is the matter?" I'd never seen him look so down.

"I'm sorry to bother you, Jill, I just didn't know who else to talk to."

"Have a seat. Can I get you a drink?"

"Not for me, thanks."

"What's happened?"

"Maria has called it off."

"What? When?"

"Last night, totally out of the blue."

"Did she say why?"

"She gave me the 'it's not you, it's me' speech, which presumably means it is me, but I honestly don't know what I did wrong. I can usually tell if there isn't a spark, but there was—I could feel it."

"You seemed such a good match."

"We were—we are. That's what's so baffling. I can't even try to sort it out because she isn't taking my calls, and I don't know where she lives."

Poor Luther. I felt so sorry for him.

"I could have a word with her, if you like?"

"But you don't know where she lives either."

"Have you forgotten I'm a P.I?"

He managed a weak smile. "Do you think it would do any good?"

"Maybe, maybe not, but what do you have to lose?"

"Okay, thanks." He started for the door, but then hesitated. "I always hoped you and I might get around to dating, but you never seemed interested."

My mouth opened, but no words came out.

"Thanks, again, Jill," he said, on his way out.

I sat there for several moments trying to compute what I'd just heard. Luther Stone had wanted to date me? How could he have thought I wasn't interested? I had practically thrown myself at him.

***

Discussing Maria had reminded me that I still hadn't sorted out the problems next door at I-Sweat. The first time I'd tried, I'd almost ended up in hospital after falling off the treadmill. The second time, I'd been distracted when I'd seen Maria buying blood. There was a free lifetime membership at stake, so I needed to get it sorted.

Then I had a brainwave.

I took out a piece of paper, and scribbled a note.

"Is Brent in?" I asked at the I-Sweat reception desk.

"I'll just get him for you."

"Jill? Do you have news for me? Those guys were in again yesterday."

It looked as though I'd caught him mid-workout.

"Sorry, I've been really busy." I handed him the slip of paper. "The next time they come in, give them this note. I doubt you'll have any problems after that."

He read it aloud, *"Daisy Flowers is watching you. You have been warned."* "Who's Daisy Flowers?"

"I'm afraid I'm not at liberty to tell you that. Just pass them the note, and I'm pretty sure you won't see them ever again."

"Okay." He looked doubtful. "I'll give it a go."

***

I'd asked Archie Bald to meet me at his factory.

"Have you worked out what's happening, Jill?"

"I think so. Could you ask Bob Binns to meet us in the QC department?"

"Of course." He got straight on the phone to his factory manager.

Five minutes later, the four of us were in the QC department. Jimmy Underlake didn't look happy to see us. And particularly not happy to see me.

"What's going on, Archie?" Underlake seemed less confident than the last time we'd been there.

"Jill asked for this meeting."

All eyes were on me now.

"I'd like to check one of the washing machines which has already gone through QC and has been sealed, please."

"Didn't you do that the last time you were here?" Binns said.

"She checked three of them." Underlake sounded indignant. "And they were all fine."

"I'd still like to take another look—just one machine this time."

"Go ahead." Archie Bald nodded.

I walked over to the line of machines which were awaiting despatch. "This one should do."

"Remove the packaging, would you Jimmy?" Archie said.

Underlake looked unimpressed, but did as he was asked. "See, the seal is in perfect condition. Just like the others you looked at."

"Jill?" Archie looked at me.

I slipped the small, clear plastic container from my pocket, and placed it on the bench. "This, gentlemen, is the Flexilis Beetle."

"I can't see anything," Binns said.

"Look closer. They're very small."

Archie and Binns both stooped down to get a closer look.

"I don't understand," Archie said.

"Perhaps we should ask Jimmy to explain." I turned to Underlake.

By now, all the colour had drained from Underlake's face.

"Have you lost your voice, Jimmy? I'll help you out." I picked up the plastic container. "This little fellow has a staple diet of rubber. He just can't get enough of it. Jimmy here is a big fan of these little creatures. In fact, he keeps a supply of old tyres in his back garden just to feed them, don't you, Jimmy?"

Underlake said nothing, so I continued, "If you take a look inside the drum." I pointed to the washing machine that Jimmy had just unsealed. "I'm sure you'll find a number of this guy's little friends. It's easy for Jimmy to place the bugs inside the drums before the machines are sealed. No one would ever spot them unless they were looking for them. As soon as the bugs become hungry they make a meal of the rubber seal. And the best part is, the first wash will flush them away, so no one will ever see them. Ingenious, really."

"What's this all about, Jimmy?" Archie challenged him.

"You asked for it, Archie!" Underlake spat the words. "That job was supposed to be mine. You all but promised it to me."

"Pack up your things, and get out of here!" Archie pointed to the door. "And think yourself lucky I'm not going to call the police."

Underlake said something under his breath, scowled at me, and then pushed past us.

"I would never have believed it," Archie said, once Underlake had left. "He's been with me for years."

"I'm surprised you decided not to call in the police," I said.

"When I appointed Bob as factory manager, I should at least have explained to Jimmy why I'd overlooked him. I didn't, and that's on me. I owe him this much."

"What will you do now?" I asked.

"We'll have to recall all the machines from the shops, get rid of the bugs and replace the seals. But at least now we know what was causing the problem. All thanks to you, Jill. I'll never be able to thank you enough."

***

While I was in Candlefield, I decided to pop into Cuppy C. I wanted to check the arrangements for the upcoming trip to London. And while I was there, I would treat myself to a muffin.

What? Come on. It was the least I deserved after successfully cracking two cases.

There was no sign of the twins.

"Where are they?" I asked one of the assistants.

"In the back with someone."

"Can I get a caramel latte and a blueberry muffin, please?"

"Mini?"

"Not likely."

As I took a seat at the window table, I noticed a group of young wizards and witches who had gathered outside. What were they doing? What were they waiting for?

A few minutes later, Amber and Pearl appeared from the back of the shop. The man with them had a camera slung around his neck.

"Sorry, we have to close early today." Amber began to usher the customers out of the shop.

"Sorry, you'll have to leave." Pearl snatched a half-eaten scone from someone's table.

There was much moaning and groaning as the disgruntled customers were herded out of the door.

"Oh? Hi, Jill," Amber said. "I didn't realise you were here."

"What's going on? Why are you closing early?"

"We're not," Pearl said. "We're having a brochure designed, so we need the place to look hip and happening for the photographs."

"Cuppy C? Hip and happening?"

Just then, the crowd of young people began to file into the shop, and take seats at the vacant tables.

"Who are they?" I said.

"They're from Candlefield Model Agency. Our

photographer hired them for the shoot. They're more the kind of image we're going for."

"Let me see if I've got this straight. You're having a brochure designed to attract more customers?"

"Correct."

"And you've just upset your existing customers by throwing them out so you can do the shoot for the brochure?"

"It's more complicated than that." Amber corrected me. "We're trying to attract a certain class of customer. Not just anyone."

"I see. Well, I hope you know what you're doing."

"Of course we do." Pearl picked up my cup.

"I haven't finished with that."

"We need your table for the shoot."

"I could stay. I'm young and hip."

They both dissolved into laughter.

Chapter 25

It was Saturday. Jack was going bowling, and I was going to the new mall with Kathy and Lizzie—big whoop!

"Have you been to the new mall before, Auntie Jill?" Lizzie had brought a beanie ghost with her.

"Yes, have you?"

"No, but Mummy has. She says it's brilliant."

"Your mummy is easily impressed."

"You could at least pretend to be excited, Jill," Kathy said in a hushed voice so Lizzie wouldn't hear.

"I am. Look at this face. This is my excited face."

"You'd better not spoil it for Lizzie."

"I won't. When did she get the new beanie?"

"Last week. She's decided to start collecting all things ghost related."

"It's a step up from the Frankenstein beanies, I suppose."

"We're here!" Lizzie pointed.

"The shark has gone," I said.

"What shark?" Kathy gave me a puzzled look.

"The giant shark that was above the entrance. You must have seen it?"

"I can't say I noticed."

There were two young men, dressed in red uniforms, just inside the entrance.

"Excuse me." I tapped the young man's shoulder. "What happened to the shark?"

"Which shark, madam?"

Lizzie had obviously inherited her mother's shopping genes. Between the two of them, they dragged me into every clothing, shoe, and toy shop in the mall.

"I'm starving," I moaned, after we'd been there for the best part of a month.

"We've only just got here." Kathy was checking the store directory, just in case we'd missed any of the clothes shops.

"It's a quarter to twelve. I'm starving. If we go now, we'll beat the rush."

"Are you hungry, Lizzie?" Kathy asked.

"Yes. Can I have pizza, Mummy?"

We headed for the food court where Lizzie and Kathy ordered pizza. I had a baked potato with cheese topping.

"Ladies, gentlemen and children." The voice came over the large speakers, which were scattered around the food court. "Today, we are proud to announce a new feature, called Five Minute Stories, here at Central Mall. Throughout the day, a number of storytellers will read short stories for your entertainment. Please give a warm welcome to the first storyteller of the day, Witch Anastasia. She'll be reading a story entitled 'The Hidden Passageway'."

The crowd in the food court applauded, as a woman dressed in what looked remarkably like genuine witch attire, took to the small stage.

"Thank you, everyone," she said. "And a special thank you to all you children. I hope you enjoy the story."

Lizzie and Kathy seemed enthralled.

Did you notice how I'd added that word to my vocabulary?

Anastasia continued, "This story is about a witch named Julia. Now, children, don't worry because Julia was a good witch, not an evil witch. One day, Julia was summoned to a castle many miles from her home. This castle was surrounded by high walls, which had been built to keep out all the scary creatures that lived in that region. While the witch was in the castle, one of the creatures broke through the wall, and snatched a young boy."

This story seemed somehow very familiar.

Anastasia read on, "It seemed like the creature would escape with the boy, and take him back to its nest, to eat him."

The children all gasped in horror.

"Don't worry, children. Julia knew of a secret passageway which allowed her to head off the creature, and save the boy. Everyone hailed her a hero, but she was confused. Julia couldn't understand how she had known about the secret passageway because she'd never been to the castle before. This worried her for a long, long time, but then a stranger told her that the answers she was seeking would begin with a book, which was at the bottom of a deep, dark well."

Just then, there was a loud bang, and a puff of green smoke appeared where the storyteller had been sitting. When the smoke cleared, there was no sign of her.

"Err—I'm sorry about this." The man, who was making the announcements over the speakers, sounded just as puzzled as everyone else. "We seem to have lost Witch Anastasia. Never mind. There'll be another Five Minute Story in half an hour."

"That was a rubbish story," Lizzie complained.

"It was," Kathy agreed.

I was too stunned to speak.

***

After we'd finished lunch, I made an excuse to leave. I was pretty sure that Kathy didn't believe my complaints of an upset stomach, but she didn't challenge me in front of Lizzie.

Grandma was on the roof terrace, sunbathing.

"Look what the cat's dragged in," she greeted me. "You know Agatha, I believe?"

I'd been so preoccupied with my thoughts that I hadn't noticed my cleaner, Agatha Crustie, lying on the next sun lounger.

"Oh, hi, Agatha. I didn't see you there. Grandma, there's something I need to talk to you about."

"I'm listening."

"In private."

"Agatha and I are chatting."

"It's alright, Mirabel." Agatha stood up. "It's time I was going."

"What's so top secret?" Grandma said, once Agatha had left.

"I need your advice."

"You're asking for my advice? That's a first."

"Something weird is going on."

"Isn't weird the new normal in your life?"

"I suppose it is, but this is even stranger than usual."

"Go on. I'm listening."

"Did you see the interview I did on Candle Investigates?"

"I never watch that rubbish."

I brought Grandma up to speed on the incident at

CASS.

"You knew about a hidden passageway? Is that what all the fuss is about? You're a powerful witch. Maybe your magic sensed the different thickness of the wall?"

"But I wasn't even thinking about a passageway. Anyway, that's not all. There's the business with Imelda Barrowtop. She thought I was Magna Mondale."

"That doesn't mean anything. Imelda was probably hallucinating."

"She left me a journal in her Will."

"I didn't know that. What's in it?"

"I don't know because I can't claim it unless I produce Magna Mondale's book."

"That's at the bottom of the Dark Well, isn't it?"

"Yes. What do you think I should do?"

"You'd better get that book back."

"How am I supposed to do that?"

"You'll figure it out."

Good talk!

***

I couldn't wait to get home, to put my feet up. I planned to spend the evening watching bad movies, eating chocolate and drinking ginger beer.

When I walked through the door I could hear voices. Jack was speaking to someone — a woman.

"Susan?"

Susan Bestwick was sitting on the sofa.

"Hi, Jill. I popped over on the off-chance you'd be in. As I said on the phone, I like to take a photograph of all my sculptures."

"Why didn't you tell Susan that you'd broken it, Jill?" Jack said.

"It's okay," Susan said. "These things happen."

"I'm really sorry, Susan. I didn't have the heart to tell you."

"Don't give it another thought. I always keep the pattern for every sculpture I make, so it's no problem for me to cast another one for you."

"That's brilliant news, isn't it Jill?" Jack said.

"Brilliant, yeah."

"She's going to put it on the mantelpiece, next to my bowling trophy, aren't you, Jill?"

"On the mantelpiece. Yeah."

Oh bum!

ALSO BY ADELE ABBOTT

The Witch P.I. Mysteries:

Witch Is When... (Books #1 to #12)
Witch Is When It All Began
Witch Is When Life Got Complicated
Witch Is When Everything Went Crazy
Witch Is When Things Fell Apart
Witch Is When The Bubble Burst
Witch Is When The Penny Dropped
Witch Is When The Floodgates Opened
Witch Is When The Hammer Fell
Witch Is When My Heart Broke
Witch Is When I Said Goodbye
Witch Is When Stuff Got Serious
Witch Is When All Was Revealed

Witch Is Why... (Books #13 to #24)
Witch Is Why Time Stood Still
Witch is Why The Laughter Stopped
Witch is Why Another Door Opened
Witch is Why Two Became One
Witch is Why The Moon Disappeared
Witch is Why The Wolf Howled
Witch is Why The Music Stopped
Witch is Why A Pin Dropped
Witch is Why The Owl Returned
Witch is Why The Search Began
Witch is Why Promises Were Broken
Witch is Why It Was Over

The Susan Hall Mysteries:
Whoops! Our New Flatmate Is A Human.
Whoops! All The Money Went Missing.

AUTHOR'S WEB SITE
http:www.AdeleAbbott.com

FACEBOOK
http://www.facebook.com/AdeleAbbottAuthor

MAILING LIST
(new release notifications only)
http:/AdeleAbbott.com/adele/new-releases/